Pledged to the Wolf

Reformed Rogues, Volume 3

Elina Emerald

Published by Elina Emerald, 2021.

Table of Contents

Copyright 1
Dedication 2
Prologue 3
Chapter 1 – The Search for a Wife 4
Chapter 2 – Precious Cargo 20
Chapter 3—Pledged 34
Chapter 4–When the Wolf's Away 52
Chapter 5 - Homecoming 65
Chapter 6—A Marriage in Truth 77
Chapter 7–French Connection 85
Chapter 8–The Past 96
Chapter 9 - The Letters 105
Chapter 10 – Half-Truths 119
Chapter 11 - Suspicion 131
Chapter 12–Ending Things 147
Chapter 13 - Decisions 161
Chapter 14—The MacGregors 168
Chapter 15—She-Wolf 177
Chapter 16 - The Wolf 193
Chapter 17–The Intervention 200
Epilogue 211

Copyright

Copyright ©2021 by **Elina Emerald**

Pledged to the Wolf Publisher Elina Emerald. All rights reserved. No part of this publication may be reproduced, distributed, or transmitted in any form or by any means, including photocopying, recording, or other electronic or mechanical methods, without the prior written permission of the publisher, except in the case of brief quotations embodied in critical reviews and certain other non-commercial uses permitted by copyright law. For permission requests, contact via links; info@elinaemerald.com or www.elinaemerald.com/books[1]

Cover design by 100covers

Note: This is a work of historical fiction. Depictions of real historical figures, places and events are largely fictitious.

---

1. http://www.elinaemerald.com/books

Dedication

To my big, boisterous and loving family...

Prologue

1043 River Tay, Scotland

Dalziel Sidheag Robertson, otherwise known as *'The Wolf,'* had witnessed much death in his thirty-two years on earth. Most of it was administered by his own hand.

As the Red King's assassin, he wielded his daggers with precision. A silent, deadly force. None of his targets saw or heard him coming until it was too late.

His identity had remained a closely guarded secret, as his legend grew in notoriety.

Being marked by *the Wolf* was akin to being marked by the devil himself. Such was the fear he evoked.

But someone other than his brothers and closest contacts now knew his secret.

Dalziel stared down at the bloated corpse lying beside the *River Tay*. He held a cloth over his nose to prevent the stench from seeping into his pores. This was the third *Angles* contact who was murdered before Dalziel could speak to him.

The murderer left another perfumed note written in French. It was pinned to the man's clothing. The message the same as the previous ones.

"Je me sens seul. Louve"- I'm lonely. She-wolf

Dalziel clenched his jaw in anger. He vowed whoever *'She-wolf'* was, he would do everything in his power to eliminate the threat.

Chapter 1 – The Search for a Wife

Stanhope Estate, Bamburgh, Northumbria

This whole wife hunting business was giving Dalziel a headache. But he had no choice. He was in Northumbria now. A place he detested, on a mission for King Macbeth, and he needed to shackle himself to an English wife with exacting specifications so as not to arouse suspicion.

Like everything else in his life, it all came down to precision. Or you were dead.

Dalziel turned to his chamberlain and clerk, Rupert, and asked, "How goes the search?"

Rupert replied, "I have found some women who could meet your requirements."

Mrs. Armstrong, Dalziel's Scottish housekeeper, walked in with a tea tray and began setting refreshments out for the men. "What requirements would those be, me lord?" she asked.

Dalziel replied, "I want a quiet woman above reproach, excellent reputation. Plain and unobtrusive. Twould be preferable if she had a brain in her head and I want her to behave and dress respectably.

"You forgot to mention *walks on water and performs miracles* as well." Mrs. Armstrong smirked as she continued serving tea.

Dalziel gave her a stern look, which she ignored as she placed a scone on his plate.

Rupert said, "I've narrowed the list of contenders to five such women."

"With criteria like that, I'm surprised ye found any," Mrs. Armstrong muttered under her breath.

Dalziel scowled at his impertinent housekeeper and bit into his scone, then tried not to groan because it was delicious. She had topped it with his favorite potted cream and jam preserve. He realized that was the only reason he put up with her, and the blasted woman knew it because she gave him a smug smile.

"First name on the list?" Dalziel asked Rupert after he inhaled his scone and gestured for Mrs. Armstrong to serve him another.

"Delia Crawford, nineteen—"

"Too young. Next," Dalziel interrupted.

Rupert moved down the list. "Abigail Foster, two and twenty…"

"Go on."

"Daughter of a Baron, currently widowed."

"Widowed? So young?" Dalziel inquired.

"Her beau fought in the Welsh Battle at *Rhyd Y Groes* and never returned."

Dalziel filed that information away and asked, "Character traits?"

"Quiet, pleasant, although there is a hint of scandal."

"What kind of scandal?" Dalziel raised his brow.

"'Tis rumored she had an affair with—"

"Next," Dalziel said.

Rupert continued. "Mary Trench, three and twenty, daughter of a peer, biddable, quiet, no scandal."

"Finances?"

"Independently wealthy, attractive, many suitors vying for her han—"

"Next. I dinnae want to be calling out love-sick beaus." Dalziel dismissed yet another contender.

"Harmony Durham, four and twenty, daughter of a merchant, excellent reputation, quiet—"

"And thick as two planks of wood." Mrs. Armstrong snorted, then realized she had spoken aloud. She quickly made her way out the door.

Dalziel rubbed his forehead. "Continue," he said.

"There is no more, my lord. This is the fifth list where you have rejected every prospective bride, but I can keep searching."

Dalziel sighed. "Aye, please do. There has to be *someone* in this blasted shire who satisfies my conditions."

Sometime later, after Rupert left, Dalziel was sitting in his study when Mrs. Armstrong hovered in the doorway. "Might I suggest something me lord?"

"Would it make any difference if I said no?" Dalziel asked.

"None whatsoever," she replied as she strode across the room and took a seat.

"Do make yourself comfortable, Mrs. Armstrong," he said sarcastically.

"Thank ye, I shall. Now then." She sat forward as if imparting some secret wisdom. "I think ye have been going aboot this wife hunting the wrong way. Ye need to go out into society and meet women to judge for yourself."

"Mrs. Armstrong, I dinnae have time to prance about searching for a wife. Tis why I pay Rupert to do it for me. Macbeth wants me back in Scotland. My chieftain needs me back in Scotland and I cannot let them down."

"Who chooses your horses, me lord?" Mrs. Armstrong changed tack.

"I do."

"Why is that? Why not pay someone else to find them for ye?"

"Because horses are a tremendous investment. I ken what I want, and I am an expert on horseflesh."

"Surely a wife is an even greater investment, and unless ye want to put her in the stables with the horse, she will live in this house alongside ye. Would ye not want to make sure ye choose the right one?"

"She may live here, but I dinnae intend to spend any time with her. I have enough trouble in Alba to contend with."

"So, ye would trust a stranger ye ken nothing aboot, to live here, among all your secretive things?" She waved her hand about his study. "While you hie off to the Highlands?"

Dalziel thought about it. It would be remiss of him not to at least scrutinize his future wife before deciding. Maybe it was something he needed to do himself.

"Aye, point taken, Mrs. Armstrong. I'll speak to Rupert to arrange a dinner where I can meet these ladies."

Mrs. Armstrong grinned. "Tis settled then."

"What is?"

"There's an assembly held by the ealdormen in town tonight. I prepared your bath and clothes in your chamber. The stable boy has already brought your horse around and Mr. Rupert will meet ye there." She took her leave.

Dalziel watched her disappear down the hallway before he chuckled and shook his head. *Mrs. Armstrong should be an assassin.*

Driftwood Cottage, Bamburgh, Northumbria

CLARISSA HARCOURT DUG her hands in the dirt and pulled out more potatoes. "Yes!" she shouted in defiance. "We shall eat a veritable feast tonight, Ruth." She grinned at her cook.

"Where are yer *shoon*?" Ruth asked.

"You know I dislike wearing shoes. I prefer to feel the grass under my toes and the wind in my hair," Clarissa replied, doing a quick pirouette in the dirt.

"And the ague in your bones if ye're not careful," Martin, Ruth's husband, said while pulling out more potatoes.

"Tis not a done thing to be roaming about the countryside like a wee sprite." Ruth admonished.

"Now Ruth, you flatter me, but I am not a sprite. My hips are too wide." Clarissa responded with a wink.

The couple laughed. They were in their fifties and had been with Clarissa's family for years. They were the last remaining servants who stayed on after Clarissa and her brother Cedric had inherited a mountain of debt from their late father.

"Ruth, mayhap you can make us a tasty potato pie?"

"I can do that, Mistress," Ruth replied cheerfully, "and we can add some cabbage to it."

Clarissa glanced at the lifeless cabbage Ruth was holding up and tried not to grimace.

She turned to Martin and asked, "How did you get on at the docks?"

"There is still no word on the shipments or Cedric. Something does not feel right," Martin replied.

"I agree. We have never gone this long without a word before. If something is not done soon, we will have to move our precious cargo and find some much-needed funds."

Martin said, "I have asked at the mill, and they've agreed to take me back on half-pay if I apologize. It willna be much, but it will tie us over until we hear from Cedric."

"Absolutely not, Martin. That mill owner is a cheating sack of coo dung! You should not apologize for calling him out on it." Clarissa stood and wiped her hands on her apron. "I still have pieces of jewelry I can sell to get us out of this bind." Clarissa touched the gold chain around her neck. It was all she had left of her mother, but she could not be sentimental when they were about to starve to death.

"Mistress ye cannot sell yer ma's precious necklace, tis all ye have to remember her by," Ruth exclaimed.

"Memories will not feed us, Ruth. We need to eat, and we need to survive. Others depend on us now. Let us pray that the good lord above delivers up a miracle."

No sooner had she spoken than she saw the unwelcome sight of someone approaching. Clarissa abandoned all thoughts of food, looked towards the house, and cringed.

Ruth and Martin moved closer to stand behind her. No doubt for support.

"Ah, Mr. Snape, what a surprise to see you," Clarissa said in greeting.

Edmund Snape was a wealthy merchant and the *tithing-man* for their collective. It was his role to ensure each family contributed their share to the common group. He was a lanky coxcomb with a skeletal frame and greasy blond hair. Clarissa knew he was there to collect their debt. There was no way she could pay it. Not after the lean winter and the added expenses.

Snape ran his beady eyes the length of Clarissa. She schooled her features even as he lingered too long upon her chest.

"I am here to collect your contribution." He spoke with a hissing voice.

To Clarissa, he sounded like a snake. *Snape the snake*. She repeated in her head before saying, "Mr. Snape, as I have discussed with you before, I must await my brother Cedric. Tis he who oversees our family contribution."

Snape was skeptical. "What about the *frankpledge*? If tis not paid, the whole collective will suffer. I will have to involve the shire-reeve in the matter."

Clarissa hid her emotion. The last thing she needed was a Reeve and law enforcer poking about their business. "Please Mr. Snape, tis unnecessary to involve anyone, I just need more time. My brother—"

"We all ken your brother has abandoned you." Snape hissed.

"Tis not true. Cedric will be home soon, and he will set things to rights." Clarissa was trying to keep her anger in check. She hated Snape. Clarissa could easily crush his windpipe if she wanted to, but that would only attract unwanted attention and discretion was key.

Snape leaned in and whispered in her ear, his fetid breath brushing against her neckline. "Ye know my terms. Ye need only warm my bed and I'll cover the debt."

Martin was raising his fist to punch Snape, but Clarissa stayed his hand and stepped back. "Thank ye for your kind offer, Mr. Snape, but I must decline."

"Ye'll come around soon. I always get what I want, Clarissa…"

"She's Miss Harcourt to you, you *skamelar*!" Ruth angrily bit out.

He laughed out loud. "You think yourselves better than us, but look at ye now, just poor sods playing in the dirt." With those words, he stomped on the potatoes with his shoe, crushing them into the ground.

Clarissa stared in horror at the remnants of what would have been their supper.

Snape's eyes raked her once over and he said, "Ye have a *sennight'* or ah'll be collecting your debt another way. Enjoy your supper, *Miss Harcourt*," he sneered, then left.

When he was no longer in sight, Ruth asked, "What are we going to do, Mistress?"

"We need to find Cedric. I'll speak to Harmony tonight, mayhap she has heard from him. I know he loves her and if there is anyone, he would contact it would be her," Clarissa replied.

"But she'll be at the town assembly, tis too risky to talk of matters there."

"Do not fret Ruth, I'll bathe and wear my best dress so I can blend in." Clarissa turned to Martin and asked, "Can you accompany me into town?"

"Aye Mistress, of course," he replied.

Town Hall, Bamburgh

FROM THE MOMENT DALZIEL entered the assembly, several women and their mothers accosted him. It would appear everyone was expecting him and eager to make his acquaintance.

"What the devil did you tell these people, Rupert?" He tried to feign a smile while talking through gritted teeth.

"I just let it be known you are a wealthy Thane from the Highlands, and you desperately need a suitable wife."

"You did what?" Dalziel frowned. "How the hell can I meet anyone if I keep getting attacked by women with embroidered handkerchiefs?" He plucked out several surreptitiously tucked into his coat and dropped them on the floor.

Rupert just shrugged.

It was an hour later when Dalziel could finally extricate himself from a group of marriage-minded mothers and their desperate offspring. He quickly made his way out to the hallway to get some fresh air.

That was when he saw her.

She had vibrant colored auburn hair tied back in a severe bun, although the curls seem to struggle for freedom. Her eyes were green and glittered like emeralds. She stood against a wall beside a woman with raven black hair and they appeared to be talking in urgent whispers.

He thought her unremarkable. Her clothing was modest and her face unpainted. Average height, nicely curved and rather plain, but those eyes captured his attention. They sparkled with intelligence and amusement despite the serious frown on her face.

He began circling.

Dalziel asked Rupert, "Who is that woman?"

"Clarissa Harcourt."

"Husband?"

"None."

"Why was she not on the list?" Dalziel asked.

"I thought her a bit too long in the tooth."

"How old?"

"Eight and twenty," Rupert replied.

Dalziel was glad she was closer to his age. "What of her family?" he asked.

"Father was a Marquess, her mother was a foreigner, merchant class." Rupert turned up his nose at the word foreigner. "She has one brother, although no one has seen him, for some time."

Dalziel kept watching Clarissa and her friend. Both women were becoming agitated about something.

"What is she like?"

"Wallflower, boring, horrendous to be around."

"How do you ken that?"

"Tis just what most gentlemen say about her, especially ones who have tried to woo her in the past. Lord Chamberlain and Lord Lancet over there." Rupert nodded towards the two men on the other side of the Hall. "They say she is dull as ditchwater."

"I see. And the woman beside her?" Dalziel asked.

"That is Harmony Durham. She was on the list you rejected."

"Ah, the one Mrs. Armstrong believes to be a dunce. How do they ken each other?"

"Alas, my lord, I know nothing more about Miss Harcourt other than what I have told you."

"Then I shall have to find out for myself. Introduce me." Dalziel nudged Rupert with his elbow.

"My lord?" Rupert stammered, slightly taken aback.

"I'd like to ken her better, see if she is suitable. Introduce me."

"But... but surely there are—?"

"There are what, Rupert?"

"Prettier... younger, options."

Dalziel felt affronted by Rupert's words and glared. "Rupert, I suggest you stop degrading my potential *future* wife before you find yourself unconscious on the floor."

"So sorry, forgive the impertinence. I will organize an introduction at once."

Dalziel watched Rupert make his way across the crowded room, but before Rupert reached the woman in question, she had inched her way to a side entrance and disappeared.

Clarissa

SO THAT WAS THE WILD Highlander. Clarissa felt unnerved by the meticulous attention he was paying her, but she ignored it.

When she had come to the assembly, her only thought was to get word to Harmony then leave. But everywhere she turned, all anyone could talk about was a mysterious Scottish thane in want of a wife. Then, when he entered the room, Clarissa held her breath in astonishment. He was the most handsome man she had ever seen, and he vibrated raw, virile energy until it was overwhelming.

He towered above the other men and wore expensive English attire. The way he filled his clothes, especially his trews with strong lean thighs, made other men seem like spineless nothing.

He had long blonde hair parted and braided on both sides with leather ties through the braids and leather bands on his wrists. His hands were large and rugged, not soft and effeminate like other men, and his skin had been kissed by the sun. He made her heart race.

When he scanned the room, she leaned back into the shadows along the wall and observed him from the safety of her vantage point. He reminded her of a predator. He did not walk he stalked, and his keen assessing eyes missed nothing.

Clarissa felt a slight pang of jealously when he was approached by so many beautiful women. She glanced down at her shabby dress and shook her head. Clarissa was no young miss in bloom, and her outfit, once the height of fashion, was now outdated by several seasons. She was far too plain and poor to interest such a man.

Melancholia settled over her once more. She needed to stop these fanciful thoughts. There were much more important matters to attend to. People's lives were at stake, and she had to get this done and leave.

Clarissa focused on her brother's sweetheart, Harmony. She always had to break matters down for Harmony because, as passionate as Harmony was for the *Cause*, she was not very bright.

"Harmony, have you heard any word from Cedric? Anything at all? Even about the shipments?"

"No, nothing, not even a letter. I am most upset that he has shown no regard for my fragile feelings." Harmony pouted.

"Then we must change our plans. I will be at the docks tomorrow night and if anyone asks about Cedric, please tell them you have seen him at your townhouse, and he is well."

"But I have *not* seen him, Clarissa. I thought that was what we just established." Harmony stared at her like she was daft.

Clarissa was growing frustrated. She often wondered what Cedric saw in Harmony because, after two minutes in her company, Clarissa wanted to bludgeon her to death. "*I* know that, and *you* know that, but the shire-reeve does *not* know that. He has been keeping watch over our movements," Clarissa explained.

"Oh, so you need me to lie for you and pretend that I have seen Cedric?"

"Yes, just this once, and I'll never ask it again. I would not even ask it now if I did not have the *tithing-man* breathing down my neck. Until I find Cedric, people need to believe he has not abandoned the *Cause*."

"And this will help the *Cause*?"

"Yes, it will, Harmony. Please, just do this one thing."

Harmony twirled her hair with her finger, then nodded. "All right, Clarissa. I shall be proud to lie on your behalf." She giggled.

Clarissa sighed. These were desperate times. "Thank you, Harmony, but please try not to tell people you're lying."

"Oh, of course not, tis our secret." Harmony tapped her nose and winked twice.

When Clarissa glanced around the hall, she noticed the Highlander had moved and was now speaking to someone else. They were both glancing in her direction. She stared at a distant point in the ceiling so as not to make eye contact.

"Can I dance now?" Harmony asked.

"Aye, of course. Thank you again," Clarissa replied.

Harmony smiled. "Tis my pleasure."

They parted ways. Clarissa slipped through the side entrance. It was time to leave. But first, she was going to peruse the supper table. No point in having all that food go to waste.

The Supper Table

DALZIEL STALKED HIS prey from the shadows. It had taken him a while to guess Clarissa's destination, but now she was alone at the supper table, while everyone was busy dancing in the hall. He watched her covet the fare, lick her lips before she pulled out a piece of cloth, and wrapped an assortment of food in it. She then placed her haul into her reticule. It was all done in a very ladylike fashion. Anyone staring from afar would not even notice. Once her bag was full, she grabbed a tart, took a bite out of it, closed her eyes, and moaned.

Dalziel went rock hard instantly. He had never been so turned on watching a woman eat before. She ate the rest of the tart, wiped her lips discreetly, then moved away from the table.

Before he could gather his scattered thoughts, she turned and slipped out another door leading towards the stables.

CLARISSA WALKED AT a brisk pace down the dimly lit path. Her reticule was full, and the tart had taken the edge off her hunger. Her mind was already ticking on the many things she needed to accomplish. She spied Martin milling about inside the stables with the other men. She just needed to get to him, and they could leave.

Clarissa stopped in her tracks and stiffened. The hairs on the back of her neck stood on end as the looming sight of Edmund Snape stepped out in front of her to block her pathway.

"Well now, what do we have here? You're looking vera fine tonight, Miss Harcourt," he rasped.

"Thank you, Mr. Snape. I was just on my way home, but you best hurry or you'll miss the festivities inside."

Clarissa sidestepped to the right to get around him, but he moved as well and blocked her path. She sidestepped to the left, and he moved in unison.

"Please move out of my way, sir," she demanded.

"Now why would I do that when a pretty woman stands before me, begging to be taken in hand?"

Clarissa snorted while staring at Snape's effeminate, skeletal fingers. She realized her mistake when his hand shot out and gripped her wrist, pulling her towards him. His fingers dug into her skin and it hurt.

Clarissa cursed the confines of her garment. If it were not the only decent gown she had left, she would think nothing of tearing it so she could kick him in the groin. She tried to wriggle free, but he was too strong. The other alternative open to her was to drop her reticule and throat punch him, but she preferred to eat tonight and refused to risk her supper for *any* man.

"Unhand me," she said in anger. But it was no use. Snape was pulling her towards him. His other hand latched onto the back of her neck. Clarissa grimaced, knowing he was going to kiss her.

"Let go of me!" She was struggling to break free and resisted the pull. He dipped his head and was moving his narrow lips towards hers. Clarissa scrunched her eyes shut. Her only alternative was to headbutt him and possibly break his nose.

She was preparing to do just that when she heard a menacing voice in a Scottish brogue demand, "Let her go or you will die where you stand."

Snape immediately released her. Clarissa stumbled backward and came up against a solid chest. She opened her eyes and found herself ensconced within the Highlander's arm. His front to her back, one arm banded around her waist, holding her tight against his body while his other arm was outstretched. He wielded a long dagger. The sharp tip of the blade rested on Snape's neck. If Snape moved even an inch, the blade could kill him.

"Touch her again and I will kill you," Dalziel said.

Snape paled and began sweating profusely and trembling.

"Me lord, tis a misunderstanding is all," Snape replied.

Dalziel kept his eyes on Snape and asked, "What would you like me to do with this one?"

Clarissa was still reeling from the heady sensation of being held so intimately by the Highlander before it registered that he was asking her a question.

She tilted her head and stared up at his firm jawline.

"Would stabbing him in the groin be asking too much?" she asked.

Dalziel immediately glanced down and had to catch his breath as his eyes clashed with emerald-colored ones. He realized he was wrong in his earlier estimations. She was not plain at all; she was exquisite, and her eyes danced with amusement.

His face split into a wide grin, and he burst out laughing.

The movement caused the tip of his blade to nick Snape's neck and draw blood.

"Me lord!" Snape screeched. "You're cutting me."

Dalziel turned back to Snape and replied, "Och, so I am." He sheathed his dagger. "Leave now before I cut you some more."

Snape turned and ran.

Dalziel continued to hold Clarissa as they both watched Snape stumble towards his horse, trip and fall over, then get up and keep running.

Clarissa breathed in Dalziel's masculine scent. She wanted to burrow deeper into his arms, but it was a public place, and she soon came to her senses. "Thank you. I am most grateful for your help."

Dalziel leaned in closer. He wanted to keep her and bury his face in her neck. But he reluctantly released her when he felt her pull away.

Clarissa turned to face him. She appeared nervous and vulnerable. Dalziel felt the need to protect her. He wanted to feed her and make sure she never had to fill her reticule with food. That she never wanted for anything. He mentally shook himself. *What the hell was happening to him?* He could not afford to get close to anyone. *He was dangerous.*

Dalziel stepped away and put distance between them. His smile disappeared, replaced by a stony stare. He noticed her amusement faded as if a veil descended. Her face became serious as she stepped further away, taking his cue.

Dalziel wanted to pull her back into his arms, but again he berated himself for such soft emotions. He was an assassin. *His enemies were deadly.* No, he needed to stop this now. Rationalize and separate, he kept repeating to himself.

"Who was that man?" he asked.

"He is the *tithing-man*, Edmund Snape, and a neighbor. Twas a misunderstanding is all."

Dalziel was skeptical. He would gather details later.

Silence filled the space between them as they gazed at one another.

Rupert shattered the quiet. "Miss Harcourt, I see you have met Lord Stanhope. I have been searching for you both everywhere."

"Tis Dalziel Robertson, Stanhope is a mere title," Dalziel said.

"Pleased to meet you, my lord. I am Miss Clarissa Harcourt." She reached out her hand in greeting.

Dalziel instantly took it and bowed over it. "Twould seem your introductions are no longer necessary, Rupert," Dalziel grumbled.

Rupert blushed at his tardiness and the reprimand. A young woman requesting a dance had waylaid him and he forgot his task altogether.

"Do you need an escort home, lass?" Dalziel asked Clarissa.

"No, tis all right. My steward is waiting just in the stables. I should go. He will worry."

Dalziel nodded and watched her leave. A strange feeling came over him. He did not like it. He could not fathom why she had such an effect on him. Then he decided. He would *not* marry her. She made him feel too much, and what he needed was a marriage where he felt nothing. Dalziel had vowed that he would not repeat the mistakes of his father.

Nothing good ever came from loving an English woman. He should know. His mother was one, and it almost destroyed their lives. *Clarissa Harcourt was dangerous.*

Dalziel sent one of his men to ensure Clarissa made it home safely. It was the least he could do. Then he returned to the hall and tried to clear his mind of the tempting vixen.

That night Clarissa, Martin, and Ruth filled their bellies with fancy fare Clarissa had smuggled in her bag. When she slept, she dreamed of a naked Scotsman ravishing her on the dance floor.

Meanwhile, a few miles away, Dalziel tossed and turned in his bed, dreaming of a luscious auburn-haired nymph with green eyes having her way with him as he slept.

Chapter 2 – Precious Cargo

Dalziel's Study, Stanhope Estate, Bamburgh

"You do *not* want to marry Miss Harcourt?" Rupert asked.
"Aye, she is not suitable," Dalziel replied.
"But you seemed taken with her last night."
"That was last night. Today is today."
"Do you wish for me to make a new list?"
"No, I have found someone else."
"Who?" Rupert asked, surprised.
"Harmony Durham. She seems a simple sort who will fit the role nicely."
Dalziel felt the weight of Rupert's judgment. But he did not need to explain himself to anyone.
Mrs. Armstrong barged her way into Dalziel's study. "So, how did it go at the assembly, me lord?"
"I met a woman who I will call upon tomorrow with an offer."
"Are you sure you won't reconsider Miss Harcourt?" Rupert asked.
"You met Clarissa?" Mrs. Armstrong perked up and clutched her pearl necklace.
Rupert gave Mrs. Armstrong a knowing glance and said, "Not only did he meet her, but they were having a very *private* talk outside in the dark, just the two of them."
"Och, really? That is wonderful. What did she say? What was she wearing?"
Dalziel snapped, "Mrs. Armstrong, I have a pair of balls in case you failed to notice and will not be drawn into some ladies' gossip hour."

Mrs. Armstrong seemed to deflate. "No need to be crude, me lord. I just like the lass. Tis a pity about her reduced circumstances."

Dalziel wanted to ask her what she meant, but Mr. Bell, his steward, interrupted them to announce a visitor. "My lord, Mr. Arrowsmith is here to see you. He came via the alley way."

"Thank you. Send him in."

A few moments later, the imposing figure of Highlander Ewan Arrowsmith filled Dalziel's doorway. Ewan was the same height as Dalziel, with a solid build. He wore his plaid with pride and was armed with a vast array of weaponry. Arrowsmith was a spy for Macbeth and one of Dalziel's trusted contacts in Northumbria. He was also an exceptional bowyer and often disguised his activities, working in various guilds across the country. For him to seek Dalziel in daylight meant whatever message he had was important.

Rupert and Mrs. Armstrong excused themselves from the room as Arrowsmith entered and sat down. Dalziel poured them both a dram of whiskey and shut the door.

"What news have you?"

"There has been another murder and another note," Arrowsmith said with a Scottish lilt to his baritone voice.

"Damn it to hell," Dalziel cursed and began pacing the room. "When?"

"Last night. One of my men met a servant of Earl Siward. We found him at the docks this morning with his throat slit and the French message pinned to his shirt."

"What led him to seek this servant?" Dalziel asked.

"Rumor is Siward is siding with Malcolm of Cranmore and making moves to force a war with Macbeth. An ambush of sorts."

"Any news of this servant now?"

"Vanished."

"Male or female?"

"Female."

"Something is off about all of this. Someone kens our every move before we even make it," Dalziel said. "Which leads me to believe…"

"The enemy is one of our own." Arrowsmith finished his sentence for him.

"Aye," Dalziel replied. "We should make inquiries at the docks tonight. Someone must have seen or heard something."

Arrowsmith nodded in agreement.

Dalziel changed the subject and asked, "What do you ken of a *tithing-man*, Edmund Snape?"

"Cunning, unscrupulous coward," Arrowsmith replied, then downed the shot of whiskey. "Why do you ask?"

"I caught him trying to attack a young lady last night."

"The bastard! Which lady?"

"Clarissa Harcourt. Do you ken her?"

"I've seen her about town. She is a quiet one. Keeps to herself but I've always thought her vera bonnie with nice curves."

Dalziel growled. "You've been staring at her curves, have you? You think she's bonnie, do you?" He glared at Arrowsmith.

"Depends."

"On what?"

"On whether you're going to hit me if I say aye." Arrowsmith gestured towards Dalziel's clenched fists, which were primed for a fight.

Dalziel immediately relaxed. He was not sure what had come over him, but hearing Arrowsmith, the braw bastard, talk about Clarissa's curves made him see red.

"Mayhap we should discuss the docks and stay clear of discussing your woman for now."

"She's not my woman," Dalziel snapped.

Arrowsmith raised his hands palm up in a show of surrender. "All right, calm down. I was only jesting." He studied Dalziel with curiosity. He had never seen the man show any kind of emotion before, especially over a lass.

Dockside, Bamburgh, Northumbria

IT WAS 2 AM, AND CLARISSA and her men were in place. With no sign of her brother Cedric, she moved their precious cargo under the cover of darkness.

They crouched beside large barrels outside the dockside brothel and waited for the coast to clear. She wore her usual attire of trews, tunic, and boots. Her normally unruly hair bound tight and pinned to a cap. All of them had their faces smudged with dirt and soot to blend in.

Jean-Luc, her cousin, disappeared inside the brothel, then came out a few minutes later with three women and two small children.

Clarissa calmed their fears as Pierre, Jean-Luc's brother, rushed them to the waiting boat.

"Where are the others?" she asked Jean-Luc.

"They will not leave for fear o' Goldie," he replied.

Goldie was a vicious Irishman. He owned the docks, and he was not a man to cross.

"What do you mean, they will not leave?" Clarissa asked with urgency. "Tis all or nothing."

"Mistress, something is not right, tis too quiet, we need to go now," Martin said. He had his eyes fixed on the brothel.

Clarissa was just about to agree when Toby, their lookout, came running around the side of the building yelling, "Go! Go!"

A distance away, she spotted five large men giving chase.

Pierre jumped into the boat and grabbed the set of oars fastened to the oarlocks. Toby ran past them. He loosened the ropes, then jumped in and took up the second pair of oars. "Get in," he yelled.

"Bugger," Martin cursed. "Mistress, they're too close. Go with others. Me and Jean-Luc will hold them off to give you a head start."

"Go Ris," Jean-Luc demanded.

"No, I am not leaving you two." There was no way she was returning to the *cove* to explain to Ruth that she had abandoned her husband at the pier.

"*Mademoiselle*, we need to go now!" Pierre shouted, already maneuvering his oars in the water.

Clarissa could see the women and children trembling in fear, and she made a split-second decision. *Precious cargo.* She bent down, pushed the boat away from the dock, and shouted at Pierre to stick to the plan. She heard him cursing at her in French, but he complied.

She then faced the attackers, took a fighting stance, and brought her fists up. "I'll take the short one on the left."

"Guess I'll take the rest then," Jean-Luc grumbled.

"What am I, chopped liver?" Martin sounded insulted.

Clarissa braced as the five men circled them. Martin did not wait he launched straight in, swinging and took down two. They were currently grappling on the ground. The other three attacked at once. Jean-Luc got one in a chokehold while fending off another. The last man headed straight for Clarissa.

He swung, and Clarissa ducked and jabbed him in the groin. She watched him wince in pain before she felt the pain explode across her cheekbone as his fist connected with her face. Clarissa cursed, knowing it would leave a bruise. She dodged the next swing he aimed at her, then she ran straight at him and pushed him hard towards the edge of the dock. He teetered before falling backward into the murky waters.

She scanned the sea; the boat was a good distance away and disappearing into the dark mist. At least that was one less thing to worry about, she thought. Clarissa ran to help Martin and Jean-Luc, who were contending with the other four. But each time she tried to get a few punches in, Martin and Jean-Luc blocked her path. *Bloody hell.* She hated it when they tried to protect her.

She did what she could between gaps and managed a few kicks and punches. She also monitored the man in the water who was trying to climb into a boat and failing miserably. His only choice would be to swim to shore and that would keep him out of their way.

~~~

Brawling

IT WAS A QUIET NIGHT at the docks as Dalziel and Arrowsmith slunk in the shadows, doing the rounds, asking questions, and handing over coins for information. They were just stepping out of an inn when they heard shouting coming from the pier.

"What is it?" Dalziel asked Arrowsmith.

"Appears to be a scuffle, four against three, and the odds dinnae favor the three. One of them is a mere lad."

"Aye, tis a most unfair fight. The other two are trying to protect him."

Arrowsmith and Dalziel did not wait. They ran towards the fighting.

"What the devil is going on here?" Dalziel yelled.

"Mind yer own fancy pants, tis nothing to do with ye," said a big burly man.

"I say different." Dalziel punched him in the jaw.

And all hell broke loose.

Clarissa could not believe her eyes when she glimpsed two Highlanders emerge from the darkness. They resembled avenging angels. She recognized them straight away. Dalziel and Arrowsmith, the bowyer from town. She stood mesmerized by their fighting style. The tide soon turned, and her attackers barely escaped with their lives.

She was so caught up in awe at Dalziel's combat abilities, she almost forgot herself.

"Bloody hell, Ris, hide!" Jean-Luc scolded her inattention.

Clarissa instantly ducked behind Martin when the attackers fled, and Dalziel headed towards her.

Dalziel asked, "Are you all right lad? You took a bit of a beating?"

Clarissa kept her head down and said in a gruff voice, "Aye, thank ye, me lord. I am hale."

Arrowsmith asked, "You sure? If you need tending lad, we can see to it." He moved towards her when Martin blocked his path.

"Tis grateful we are that ye helped us, me lords. My nephew is vera shy. Takes after me, dearly departed sister, God rest her soul. Gets nervous around strangers."

"Aye, very nervous," Clarissa grunted in a deep voice.

"Why were you set upon?" Dalziel asked.

"We'd come for a night at the brothel and for no reason these ruffians attacked us," Martin replied.

"Well, you best leave now. Tis not safe here at night. No doubt they'll be back with more men if we dally." Dalziel bid them goodnight and they left.

Martin, Clarissa, and Jean-Luc did not hesitate. They fled in the opposite direction, intending to put as much distance between them, Goldie, and the Scotsmen. They had a rendezvous at the *cove*.

The Journey Home

"TWAS IT JUST ME, OR did that lad look familiar?" Dalziel asked Arrowsmith as they rode home.

"Aye, there is something about him. I am sure I've seen him before. What did you think of his fighting style?" Arrowsmith asked.

"Full of spirit. He even landed a few good hits," Dalziel replied.

"I wonder what they were really doing down at the docks," Arrowsmith said.

"Aye. Twas like they were protecting the lad from us. No doubt it could be a member of the peerage out for a swiving and things went awry."

"I just wonder who they annoyed to earn the wrath of Goldie's men," Arrowsmith pondered out loud.

"We've probably made an enemy of Goldie now as well," Dalziel replied.

"That Irishman has always been my enemy. The fight tonight made no difference," Arrowsmith said.

Dalziel wondered what Arrowsmith meant. He knew there was a bigger story there but would not pry. Arrowsmith guarded his privacy fiercely.

As they journeyed home, Dalziel found his mind drifting to Clarissa Harcourt. He had been doing that a lot lately. He wondered what she was doing tonight and what she would think of him brawling on the dockside like a common thug. She would most likely shun him if she knew.

Still, he felt exhilarated after a good fight. Usually, he sought the company of a woman after a brawl for a hard coupling. It was probably why Lenora, his ex-mistress, had lasted so long. In his line of work, he often needed release. Lenora was one of the few women who enjoyed a bit of rough play. Dalziel found it interesting he had not seen or thought of Lenora in months, despite her attempts to rekindle a relationship.

He wondered if Clarissa could provide him the physical succor he craved after a good fight. Just the thought of her tied to his bed, naked, blindfolded, and under his complete control heated his blood. *Damn it*. He swore at himself. *Why the hell would he not get that bloody woman out of his head?*

Dalziel was even more determined to get married to Miss Durham soon and return to Scotland before his growing obsession with Miss Harcourt caused him to misstep.

The Cove

IT WAS 4AM WHEN CLARISSA reached the *cove*. They had covered their tracks well, and now they had to sit tight for a few days and wait on Cedric. Clarissa was pleased to see the women and children settled, although Pierre, the fiery head of her cousins, was furious and rained a string of expletives in French and English at her for putting her life in danger.

"If something happens to you, we lose all. You are the one who keeps things together, Ris! *You,* and no one else." Pierre's voice cracked with emotion.

"I am sorry, Cousin, truly I am. I will take better care next time." She hugged him, which seemed to appease him.

"What I want to know is how we were discovered?" Toby asked.

"Aye, twas like they were waiting for us," Martin replied.

"Goldie's men were not supposed to be there at all. Someone knew our plans," Jean-Luc added.

Clarissa's brow furrowed. The men had a point. Someone had snitched, and it nearly cost them dearly. Until she discovered who it was, they were all in danger.

Durham Town House, Bamburgh

THE NEXT MORNING, DALZIEL walked up the stairs to the large townhouse of one Harmony Durham. It was in a busy part of town, with people bustling past. He knew it was time to visit his prospective bride and hopefully formalize a pledge so he could return to his duties in Scotland.

He was admitted by a stoic butler and shown into a Drawing Room and waited.

It was not long before Harmony appeared carrying a small kitten, and he immediately regretted his decision.

"Your Lordship, Lily and I welcome you."

"Lily?"

"My kitten. Please say hello or she will feel very neglected." Harmony pouted and raised the kitten's paw to shake Dalziel's hand.

Dalziel reluctantly shook it, and the kitten bit him. He gritted his teeth and snatched his hand away.

"Aw, I think Lily likes you." Harmony giggled, oblivious to the hostile hissing stand-off that was taking place between Dalziel and Lily. "Please take a seat."

Dalziel sat and wondered how the hell he was going to get out of this situation. He had never, not once, made a misstep in any decision pertaining to the king's missions. Until now. Everything about his hasty decision made him second guess his ability to think straight.

"Have you come about Cedric?" Harmony asked.

"Who's Cedric?"

"Oh, nothing. I thought this was the part where I am supposed to explain…"

"Explain what?"

"No, wait… now I am confused. Oh, I am making a muddle of things," Harmony said with a vacant expression. "But tell me, what brings you here?"

Dalziel's instincts were screaming at him to change course. He could not go through with it and he knew it had to do with a green-eyed minx and the hissing feline now sinking its claws into his ankle.

"I had actually come to discuss the prospect of a marriage arrangement between us."

"You want to marry me?" Harmony asked, surprised.

"No, I mean yes, but before, not now," Dalziel stammered. Another thing he had never done before. Dalziel had never in his life been double-minded and unsure of himself. He had never experienced *indecision*. It was crippling.

He stood abruptly, pried Lily and her teeth from his leg, and placed her on the chair. "My apologies for the intrusion. I must leave."

He strode out of the room.

Harmony followed close on his heels. "Wait, did we just get engaged, my lord?"

"No, we did not," he clipped and marched out the front door, and kept walking.

He had just crossed the road when he saw Clarissa walking in the park a short distance away. *Speak of the devil.*

Before he thought better of it, his legs were moving in her direction. When he was closer, he called out, "Miss Harcourt?"

She spun around; her hand raised in a fist. She instantly dropped it when she saw it was just him.

Dalziel apologized. "I beg your pardon. I did not mean to startle you."

"Tis all right." Clarissa smiled. "I thought you were... someone else."

Dalziel peered down at her. Then his entire body locked. He clenched his jaw and his face filled with rage.

Clarissa took a step back. "What is the matter?"

Dalziel's hand shot out, and he cupped her chin, tilted her face to the side, and in an angry voice said, "Who. Did. This?"

Clarissa blushed. She had forgotten about her bruised cheek courtesy of the dockside brawl.

"Was it Snape? I'll kill him," Dalziel growled.

"No, twas no one. Twas an accident," Clarissa replied.

Dalziel tilted her face to the other side. "Are you hurt anywhere else?" He released her chin, then physically turned her around to inspect for himself.

Clarissa was feeling self-conscious, given the number of people milling about. She tried to slap his hands away as he turned her again, searching for visible signs of bruising.

She said, "No, my lord, but I would appreciate it if you stopped. People are staring."

"Dalziel," he said.

"I beg your pardon?" she looked confused.

"You will call me Dalziel."

"I will do no such thing, Lord Stanhope. Now will you please stop touching me tis attracting attention!"

Dalziel released her, but he did not step away. Instead, he gently brushed his knuckle across her cheek then whispered, "Who did this to you, *mo chridhe*?"

Clarissa refrained from shivering at his gentle caress. *Did he just call her 'my heart?'* His expression was pained on her behalf, and her heart melted a little.

Clarissa reached up and clasped his hand. "Really, tis nothing but an accident. I thank you for your concern, but there is no need." Her voice was a soft whisper and her message heartfelt.

They stood in silence for some time. Then Dalziel took a step back, folded his arms across his chest, his feet spaced apart taking a wide stance. "You will give me a name."

Bollocks! He would not drop it. Clarissa scrambled to make up a story, then stopped herself. *Why should she make up a story? She owed him no explanation.* She fumed that he was making demands of her when she was minding her own matters walking in a park.

"No," she replied.

"What do you mean, no?" He raised an eyebrow.

"No, is an easy enough word to comprehend. I have told you it was an accident and that should suffice."

"Well, tis insufficient," Dalziel said.

Clarissa gritted her teeth. "With respect, you are not my brother or my husband, and I do not answer to you. Good day." She moved to walk past him.

Dalziel glared at the defiant wench. She was a spitfire when angry, and she was too thin. She had dark smudges under her eyes and seemed exhausted. He remembered Mrs. Armstrong mentioning something about 'reduced circumstances,' and he did not like the thought of her suffering. He also knew the woman needed protection, and right there in the park, Dalziel decided *he* was going to be the man to take on that role. *Mine!* said that possessive voice in his head.

"Tis *Dalziel* to you, and while I may not be your brother, I have every intention of becoming your husband, so you best get used to it," he growled.

Clarissa paused and stared at him, mouth ajar.

"Now, if you will excuse me, *Clarissa*, I have matters to attend to and my clerk will be in touch."

Dalziel turned, walked away with determined steps, then yelled over his shoulder, "And I will get that name, Ris."

With those parting words, he left her standing speechless in the park not only because of his husband comment, but also because he had just called her by her nickname. Ris.

Dalziel's Study, Stanhope Estate, Bamburgh

SO, YOU'RE *not* marrying Harmony Durham now?" Rupert asked Dalziel.

"Not a chance."

"What do you want me to do with Harmony's contract?"

"Tear it up. Make a new one."

"Whose name should I place on this new one?" Rupert asked.

"Clarissa Harcourt's," Dalziel replied.

THAT AFTERNOON, DALZIEL called his most trusted staff members together to let them know his plans.

"Mrs. Armstrong and Mr. Bell, I have found a wife. I would like the chambers and solar prepared for her. When she arrives, you will both guide her in domestic matters. Rupert, you will monitor the working accounts and ensure she has adequate money for all domestic needs. I will sign off on any expenses."

Dalziel paced the floor, then continued.

"While she remains under this roof, we will accord her the proper respect as my wife. However, I expect if there is anything unscrupulous about her behavior, you will report these to me."

They all nodded in agreement.

Mrs. Armstrong was practically brimming with excitement at the prospect of a wedding. "Oh, tis exciting, me lord. So, what did the lucky lady say when ye proposed?"

"Twas not exactly a proposal," Dalziel replied.

Mr. Bell glanced at Mrs. Armstrong, who jabbed him in the side.

"Then what was it exactly?" She frowned in confusion.

"I told her I was going to become her husband and that she would hear from my clerk."

Dalziel was met with stunned silence from the three of them.

Rupert cleared his throat then asked, "So, am I to propose on your behalf?"

Dalziel replied, "Aye, you will present her with my terms. I am sure she will accept."

"Pardon me for saying so, but I really thought a man of your caliber had better wooing skills than that," Mr. Bell scoffed.

"I agree, me lord. That would have to be the most unromantic proposal I have ever heard." Mrs. Armstrong shook her head.

Dalziel replied, "I dinnae care about romance and wooing. She will agree because I will make her an offer too good to refuse."

Chapter 3—Pledged

Driftwood Cottage, Bamburgh – 'Eat'

The next day Clarissa slept in until ten am, which was late for her. She dragged her weary body out of bed, washed and dressed, then went downstairs.

She had just entered the small kitchen when she heard voices coming from the front door.

Before long, Martin and Ruth appeared excitable. "Mistress, look." They each held an enormous basket of food.

"Where did you get those?"

"Twas delivered just now. There's a note."

Clarissa read the card, and it just said, "Eat." It was signed by Dalziel. She chuckled and shook her head. *Even when giving gifts, the man was demanding.*

They unloaded the items onto the kitchen table. One basket contained salted beef, smoked ham with a jar of applesauce, pickled onions, fresh loaves of bread, and cheese, a large bag of flour, sugar, salt, and freshly baked scones, and sweetened preserves. The second basket contained eggs, butter, milk, wine, cider, some root vegetable, apples, and leafy greens.

There was enough there to keep them fed for a while, and Clarissa had never felt so grateful. The three of them practically salivated over the fare.

Ruth said, "We should make ourselves a large pot of tea and devour the scones with cream and preserves."

"And we can have ham and cheese sandwiches," Martin piped in.

"And wash it down with fresh milk!" Clarissa laughed.

Then they sobered and became quiet.

"How many people do ye think this could feed?" Martin asked.

Ruth sighed. "We could make a lot of sandwiches from this fare and a hearty broth to go with it."

"The children would love the preserves," Clarissa added.

"Bugger," Martin said. "'Twas a wonderful dream while it lasted."

Clarissa just sighed. "I suggest we make one sandwich each to fill our bellies. The rest I'll take to the *cove*."

They nodded in agreement.

Ten minutes later, the three of them gathered for a meal of one ham and cheese sandwich, each with a cup of sweet tea, and Clarissa gave thanks to the lord above for their bounty.

"I will need to thank Lord Stanhope in person for these gifts. But I wonder what he means by sending them?" Clarissa asked.

"Mayhap he's trying to fatten you up for Christmas," Ruth replied with a smirk.

"Question is, what does he expect in return?" Martin said.

That afternoon they had their answer when Rupert, Dalziel's clerk, arrived with an offer Clarissa could not in good conscience refuse.

Stanhope Estate, Bamburgh

CLARISSA SAT IN AN armchair watching the candle clock. She willed herself to remain completely still and not fidget. She took a deep breath to calm her nerves and ignored the overwhelming presence of the large Highlander, studying her from across the desk.

She could not believe she was doing this, but she had no choice. With still no word from Cedric and their *frankpledge* due, this was the best alternative to keep them all out of the poorhouse.

When the marriage offer arrived via Rupert, she was surprised Dalziel had been serious in the park and chose her to be his bride. The secret terms were agreeable to Clarissa. She was of age and did not need Cedric's consent, so she accepted.

It would be a marriage of convenience for a year and a day in name only. When it was over, she would be remunerated, and they would quietly separate whilst seeking an annulment. Once married, she would become Lady Stanhope and Dalziel would provide her with an allowance adequate to meet her needs. Dalziel had inherited his English grandfather's title.

Clarissa knew nothing of her husband's Scottish side; or why a man of property and handsome features would need to purchase an impoverished bride. These were matters she decided best left to his discretion. As long as she had funds to continue her work, the rest was trivial.

They would present a united front to the township, but in private, lead very separate lives. A part of her felt maudlin at the thought Dalziel only offered for her out of convenience, and not because of any desire or attraction he may have towards her. But she remained pragmatic.

At eight and twenty, Clarissa knew her chances for a love match and a lasting marriage had dwindled. No man would gaze upon her with desire, and she felt that deep down in her marrow. No longer in her first bloom, Clarissa had neither beauty nor wealth to recommend her and a woman in her circumstances could not afford the luxury of vanity or romantic feelings.

Dalziel emphasized the need for separate private lives, further demonstrating there was no room for physical or emotional intimacy between them and it was to be strictly a marriage in name only. She assumed that also meant he would stay out of her private life as well. This was the boon Clarissa required for the *Cause*. It was an answer to her prayers, and only a foolish woman would turn down a lucrative offer of freedom from societal strictures via a pretend marriage.

Clarissa licked her lips and her stomach grumbled as she eyed the abundant sandwich platter and scones Mrs. Armstrong had set out for them. Clarissa had not eaten since the ham and cheese sandwich the day before. She wanted to stuff every morsel in her mouth and savor the taste, but she would not ruin her comportment. Now was not the time to lose her composure. Too much rested on her ability to play her part and get this over with. If Dalziel wanted prim, proper, and dull as a stonefish, she would give it to him in spades.

Her fiancé sat across from her in complete silence as they waited for Rupert to complete the contract. Then he leaned across the table, stacked a small plate with sandwiches and scones, and pushed it towards her. In a deep voice, he commanded, "Eat."

It startled her at first. Clarissa blushed and then accepted the offering, being careful to take dainty bites while secretly groaning inside as the delicious food exploded on her taste buds.

Dalziel poured her some tea and placed the cup and saucer beside her plate. "Drink," he said. He waited until she complied with his demand before he helped himself to a scone. He sat back and put the entirety of it in his mouth and started chewing. Clarissa tried hard not to stare at his firm jawline. *Was it possible to become aroused watching a man chew food?* Her throat suddenly became parched. She watched him pour himself a cup of tea, which he skulled in one go. His large hands engulfed the tiny cup.

When they had both consumed refreshments, they sat back in complete silence again.

Dalziel was quiet, but he never took his eyes off her.

Clarissa said, "I wish to thank you for the food baskets you sent yesterday. They were much appreciated." She did not mention that it was the women and children who appreciated it.

"Tis my pleasure. I should have called in person with the fare, but I had matters in the South to attend to," Dalziel replied.

Silence descended between them once more.

Clarissa glanced at the candle clock again, realizing she was late for her next appointment and Pierre and Jean Luc would rail about her tardiness. *Bloody French were so impatient.*

"Is there somewhere you need to be?" Dalziel asked in that deep, timbred voice.

Clarissa felt a shiver run through her body each time he spoke. But she mentally shook it off.

"Ah... no." She lied.

"You seem to glance at the candle clock often. I guarantee the shadow has not moved since you last checked it."

"Oh, yes, tis a terrible habit. I like to know what the time is for..."—Dalziel stared at her, awaiting an explanation — "the dragon hour," Clarissa said. She inwardly cringed at her inability to make up an adequate lie.

"Dragon hour?" Dalziel asked.

Shut your mouth, shut your mouth. Clarissa kept saying to herself, but nope, it was too late. Once she committed to a ridiculous story, she always had to follow through. "Yes, the hour the dragons come out," she said, then wanted to bang her head against the wall. *Why could she never make up a decent tale?*

Dalziel chortled. "And what do these dragons do when they come out?"

"They capture certain types of people."

"What type of people do dragons capture?" Dalziel sat back in his chair as if settling in for a long night of entertainment.

Clarissa's mind went blank. Then she blurted out, "Virgins." She then wished for a hole to open up in the ground so she could dive in head-first and disappear.

Dalziel chuckled and reached for another scone. In between chewing, he asked, "So, these virgins that are chased by dragons. Where would they be headed this time of the day?"

Bloody hell, the man was relentless. With her back straight, Clarissa replied in a deadpan voice, "To the forest, and if you must know, tis bad luck to speak about their movements."

Dalziel grinned and stifled a laugh. His future wife was proving to be quite amusing.

Clarissa stilled and gazed at him. *Glory be, he was handsome when he smiled*; she thought. Changing the subject, she asked, "You are certain you will rarely be home when we wed?"

"Aye, there are important matters that take me away often, but the holding is in excellent hands. Should you need anything, just ask the staff."

"Is there anything you wish me to do while you are away?" she asked.

"No, you have leisure and free rein. However..." Dalziel paused.

"Yes?"

"You shall not take a lover in my absence." He stared directly at her and spoke with a firm warning.

Clarissa inhaled sharply. It was the last thing on her mind. "Of course."

"I'll not be a cuckold even if it is a marriage in name only."

"I would not dream of it," Clarissa replied.

"And you shall not be in the company of men unless I am with you."

Clarissa's spine stiffened. That was an entirely different matter which would affect her night-time activities.

Seeking clarification, she asked, "When you say the company of men, what exactly do you mean?"

Dalziel gripped his teacup. "I mean a man, any man, a group of men. You will not consort with any unless I am with you."

"That is ridiculous!" she scoffed.

"How so?" He glared at her.

"Sometimes I will need to be in the company of men to get about. Like the servants or Martin."

Dalziel sat up straight. "That's acceptable. I am talking about men of the gentry, the peerage. Some are unscrupulous and would think nothing of taking advantage of a bonnie woman whose husband is away."

It surprised Clarissa, he considered her pretty. "What if I am *seen* with men in your absence, but they were not lovers? That would not be a breach of propriety, would it?" She gave him an innocent expression.

Dalziel glared at her and made a growling sound deep in his throat. "How many men are you planning on seeing?"

"None," she squeaked. Realizing he was becoming agitated.

"Good answer."

They sat in silence again before she inquired, "And you are certain your work will take you away for long periods?"

"Aye."

Clarissa smiled in relief and only caught herself when Dalziel frowned at her.

Dalziel clenched his jaw when Clarissa seemed relieved to be out of his company. That annoyed him. Usually, women pined for his attention, but not his wife-to-be. She wanted him gone, and there was something in the way she wished it that had him feeling out of sorts.

Rupert finally entered with the contracts. He outlined all the documents she was to sign, stipulating the agreements and notifying her they had cleared all the debts to the *tithing-man* and the collective.

Clarissa stammered a shaky 'thank you' to Dalziel, and he just nodded. She wanted to say more, seeing as he had just lifted an immense burden off her shoulders, but Dalziel stared out the window.

Twenty minutes later, the contracts were signed and without pomp or ceremony, Dalziel Robertson pledged himself to Clarissa Harcourt. There would be a small wedding ceremony in the village church at the end of the week, then she would formally move in. In the meantime, she was free to do as she pleased.

Clarissa stood and shook Dalziel's hand and thanked him for his time. He refused to let it go as his eyes wandered over her face, resting on her plump lips. The moment was interrupted when a messenger arrived with a missive.

Dalziel released her hand, read the missive, and cursed. "I apologize. I would have loved to give you a tour, but I am needed in Scotland immediately. I shall return in time for the wedding." Without warning, he reached out, gently pulled her head towards his, and kissed her cheek. Dalziel lingered close, their lips mere inches apart. He stroked her cheek with his thumb. Then he dipped his head and brushed his lips against hers. It was a brief kiss, but filled with longing.

Clarissa blushed and gave him a shaky smile.

"I will hand you over to Mrs. Armstrong, who can show you around, so you become accustomed to the place. If there is anything you need, just ask, and I will provide it."

"Thank you," she whispered.

Dalziel's eyes softened. "Tis my pleasure, sweeting," he replied. Then he seemed to catch himself and stepped away abruptly. "Good day, Clarissa." He nodded, then left the room.

Mrs. Armstrong gave Clarissa a tour of the house and the connecting wood and stone structures, which made up the manor. The buildings were constructed within a large compound and fenced in. Covered walkways connected one room to another.

Mrs. Armstrong started with the bedchambers.

"Well now, the master has set aside this room for you," she said.

Clarissa glanced around in awe. It felt larger than her entire cottage. "Surely this must be a mistake?"

Mrs. Armstrong stiffened at the insult. "Why, tis not to your liking?"

"No, oh my, not at all. Tis too good, and I just assumed I would be placed elsewhere, that's all."

Mrs. Armstrong relaxed. "Not so. These are rooms for the mistress, and your solar is down the hall. The master's bedchamber is right through the dressing room and he has a connecting door."

"Oh," Clarissa said, not wanting to think about the proximity to Dalziel's bed. She wondered if he slept naked, then turned bright red and shook her head. She had to stop these salacious thoughts.

"Dinner is at six sharp. We keep early hours, but you can change that in due course to whatever suits you." Mrs. Armstrong gave her a warm smile. "Och, and the master is usually out most nights he is... away a lot," Mrs. Armstrong said almost apologetically.

Clarissa did not want to think about where the master spent his nights or with whom. It was none of her concern, although that also meant she was free to continue her nightly activities as well.

"Will you be needing a lady's maid, or any staff in particular?"

"No, tis all right. I can manage with Ruth's help."

"I have arranged private quarters for Martin and Ruth, as well."

"That is most kind of you, Mrs. Armstrong."

"They can come and go as they please. I understand they prefer to live in your cottage by the sea?"

"Yes, it remains in my family. I will maintain its upkeep."

When the tour was complete. Clarissa felt a little overwhelmed with the amount of work that went into maintaining such a large property, but she was happy she had a few days before she became Lady Stanhope. She headed to the hallway to take her leave.

As Mr. Bell, the silver-haired steward, was handing Clarissa her coat, Mrs. Armstrong asked her to wait a moment. "I have something for you. I willna be overlong."

Clarissa waited in the foyer with Mr. Bell, who stood beside the door in complete silence. She stared at the floor and tried hard not to tap her foot as the minutes ticked by. It felt like hours.

She heard someone clearing their throat and looked up to see Mr. Bell motioning with his head towards something in her coat pocket. When she glanced down, she glimpsed a note tucked in there.

"Here it tis! The master wanted you to take these." Mrs. Armstrong appeared and handed over a large basket laden with food and a platter of sandwiches.

Clarissa stared at the fare and wanted to cry when she saw the abundance of food prepared.

"Tis too much Mrs. Armstrong I could not possibly—"

"Och, tis nothing, Mistress. There is plenty to go around."

Clarissa thanked her, and without thinking, she gave her an enormous hug.

"There now, Mistress, you need not feel obliged to me." Mrs. Armstrong blushed with embarrassment but also appeared pleased. "Go on now. I see Martin is waiting outside."

Clarissa smiled and as she walked past Mr. Bell, she tapped her coat pocket and nodded to him. Then she went out to meet Martin, excited to show him her bounty. At least they would eat tonight.

The Note

WHEN CLARISSA RETURNED home, she fished out Mr. Bell's note. It was an address for an 'Elspeth Davenport' and the words, 'Tell her Silver sent you.' Clarissa did not know who the woman was, although the last name rang a bell.

That night Pierre and Jean-Luc accompanied her to the address, and it was a tiny hovel on the outskirts of the shire.

Much to the mortification of Pierre and Jean-Luc, Clarissa walked straight up to the door and knocked before they could stop her.

The door opened, and an elderly man appeared. He was guarded and viewed her with suspicion.

"What do ye want?"
"I am here to see Elspeth."
"Who sent you?"
"Silver."

He nodded, then let her into a sitting room. "Wait here."

Sometime later, he appeared again and this time he was with a woman; he was helping her walk as she limped into the room. She was covered in bruises; one eye was swollen shut. Her arm bandaged.

Clarissa took a sharp intake of breath at the extent of her bruising. The woman's eyes had the same haunting gaze her mother had after every beating.

"Who did this to you?" Clarissa asked as she moved forward to help Elspeth into a chair.

"Tis not who, but why," Elspeth replied and winced when she shifted slightly.

"What can I do?" Clarissa asked.

"You keep women safe." It was a statement, not a question.

Clarissa nodded, "Yes, I do Elspeth."

"Please called me Elsa. I need you to keep me safe, but it could place you in great danger."

Clarissa wondered what on earth Mr. Bell had gotten her into?

Dalmally, Scotland

DALZIEL CROUCHED IN the tall grass and retrieved another letter pinned to the murdered soul lying in the ditch. This contact was important. It was rumored he knew when and where Earl Siward of Northumbria would mount his attack on Macbeth.

Dalziel gritted his teeth as he read the latest perfumed message. This one was different. It said, *"Les murs ont des oreilles." - The walls have ears.*

"Damn," Arrowsmith cursed. "'Tis someone who kens our every move."

"Aye, they could be anywhere. Castles, inns, even our own homes."

"Do you ken the name of this man?" Arrowsmith asked.

"The shire-reeve said he is not from these parts, but he is hoping someone will recognize him," Dalziel replied.

"Poor sod, he didna see it coming."

"Aye, he must have kin waiting for him somewhere," Dalziel said.

"If the murderer is in our midst, then mayhap, we should spread lies about our next move. Only the culprit would act on the lie."

"Arrowsmith, you are a genius. Let's go spread some lies." Dalziel gave him a wry grin.

'The Wedding', Bamburgh

A WEEK LATER, DALZIEL stood in the village church, awaiting his bride. He had ridden hard to make it home on time. Macbeth had been pressuring him to make his marriage visible to all, so he had hastened to return.

Truth be told, he *wanted* to see his bride. Although it was a marriage of convenience, he wanted to give her a wedding day and a proper wedding feast.

For the sake of appearances, Arrowsmith stood at his side with the rings. Both men wore their Scottish plaids and leine. Dalziel donned the MacGregor crest badge and a belt with the Robertson shield. He did not notify his brothers in arms Beiste MacGregor and Brodie Fletcher or their 'interfering wives' as he called them. He did not want to involve his family at all, in a wedding which was in name only. For as long as necessary, he would keep both parts of his life separate.

A hush descended over the small crowd, and he knew his bride was approaching. What he was not prepared for was the possessive feelings he had when he saw her walking towards him.

She wore an ankle-length intricately embroidered green tunic with long sleeves and a low-cut neckline. The design accentuated her curves. A solitary gold chain was fastened around her neck. Her glorious red hair was left free and hung just below her waist, and a flowery wreath adorned the top of her head.

Dalziel held his breath. He wished so much that this was a genuine marriage, but he knew it could never be. Besides, she was English and that could not stand. He reminded himself this was a mission for the king. This could never be a proper marriage if there were only lies between them.

Clarissa greeted him with a smile, and he returned it, then reached out to clasp her hand in his. They both turned to face the priest and, in the presence of witnesses, they went through the motions of making vows neither one intended to keep.

CLARISSA COULD NOT believe this was her wedding day. A part of her was sad it was not a proper marriage, but she reminded herself it was necessary. She wished she were walking towards a man who could truly love her. But how could he when he knew nothing of her actual life? She would ensure it remained that way.

Clarissa was grateful for the dress Mrs. Armstrong provided. It had been handwoven by the finest seamstress in town, and Dalziel had also commissioned an entirely new wardrobe for his new wife. For the first time in her life, she felt like an ethereal beauty. When she viewed her husband to be, she held her breath. He was breathtakingly handsome in his Scottish attire. He stood tall and proud and when he smiled at her; she felt her heart skip a beat.

When Dalziel took her hand, it was as if an unknown energy passed between them. He gripped hers firmly and spoke his vows, loud and clear for all to hear. Clarissa pretended he meant every word, even though she knew it benefited the wedding guests.

A part of her was sad Cedric still had not returned. She would have loved for him to give her away, even if it was a marriage of convenience. As it was, only Ruth was in attendance, as Martin and her cousins were called away to the *cove*.

The ceremony was over in a relatively short time, and then it was the moment to kiss the bride.

Clarissa stared at Dalziel when he dipped his face towards her. "What are you doing?" she murmured.

"Tis time for me to kiss you?"

"In front of all these people?"

"Aye."

"I am too nervous." Her eyes pleaded for his guidance.

The innocence with which she trusted him pierced Dalziel's soul. He wanted to do more than just kiss her, but he would grant her this boon. "Dinnae worry *mo ghaol*, I'll lead."

He leaned in slightly and instructed, "Part your lips, love and breathe."

She did. He brushed his lips against hers. She responded and before Dalziel knew what he was doing; he had his arms around her as his tongue gently caressed her top lip. Clarissa wound her arms around his shoulders and met his tongue with the tip of hers. Dalziel groaned as he pulled her closer, deepening the kiss.

Both were lost in the moment. Until the sound of Arrowsmith's throat-clearing penetrated the haze. Dalziel opened his eyes and tried to calm his heavy breathing. His heart was beating out of his chest. Clarissa's lips glistened as she ran her tongue across her bottom lip, her expression dazed. The world melted away, and it was just the two of them.

Dalziel was still reluctant to let her go, until Arrowsmith muttered, "Save something for the wedding night."

Clarissa blushed, and Dalziel glowered at Arrowsmith.

The priest declared them man and wife.

Dalziel remained by Clarissa's side for the wedding feast. To all present, he played the part of a doting husband and she responded with genuine affection. Dalziel used every opportunity to caress her skin. His arm would rest behind her back or he would hold her hand if they walked to talk to guests. His fingers would brush against her nape. For a false marriage, he was very attentive towards her needs and she was glad of it.

Dalziel was proud to have Clarissa on his arm. He knew he made the right choice because she never put a foot wrong. She was a consummate hostess for all the guests and attendees. He wondered at the lack of her family and friends. Apart from Harmony, he did not know whether she had any friends. He found that strange considering she had lived in the town her whole life.

Before the guests had taken their leave, Dalziel and Clarissa retired to their chambers together. Although there would be no wedding night, they still had to keep up the pretense of being newly wedded love birds eager to consummate their marriage. So, they gave it a few hours to spend together before they moved into separate chambers.

Clarissa sat in a window nook in Dalziel's bed-chamber, reading a book.

"What are you reading?" he asked.

"Historia Ecclesiastica gentis Anglorum."

"An Ecclesiastical History of the Angles people."

His understanding of the language surprised Clarissa. "You know Latin?"

"Doesn't everyone?"

"Have you read it?"

"Of course, *Venerable Bede* is my favorite author, second only to *Pliny the Elder*." He smirked.

"I fear you are making fun of me." Clarissa gave him a skeptical look.

"Aye Wife, I am. Tis a boring tome. I dinnae ken what you find interesting in it."

She just shrugged her shoulders and continued reading.

Dalziel gazed at his wife in the fire's light, and he wished he could kiss her as he had in the church. It had taken him hours to recover from that one kiss and once he supped at her lips; he wanted to taste more. Dalziel wanted to do many things with her and to her, but he needed to control his baser instincts. He had been too long without a woman. Mayhap he would take Lenora up on her offer when he returned to the Highlands. He instantly frowned at the thought.

When the last of the guests had left and the house settled. Dalziel bid Clarissa good night and retreated to his bedchamber.

Clarissa wished Dalziel would kiss her again, but she had to remind herself this was not a genuine marriage and they could never be lovers.

Secrets We Keep

THE FOLLOWING MORNING, they both maintained their ruse ordering food to Dalziel's bedchamber before they broke their fast together. It was during this time they shared some tidbits about their lives. Dalziel told her a little about the MacGregor clan and his late father, Jacob Robertson. She noticed he had never mentioned his mother.

Clarissa talked a little of her mother but left out any mention of her father or Cedric.

She realized how much she missed her brother. This was the longest she had gone without seeing him, and now she was worried.

Both shared parts of their story but not the whole, they kept many secrets between them.

Later that night, Dalziel joined her for dinner, dressed formally in traditional Scottish attire. She wore a new blue tunic with silk brocade. Clarissa thought Dalziel even more attractive but had to force herself not to peer down at his bare knees.

Dalziel sat across from his wife, and his fingers itched to touch her. She was ravishing tonight, and the conversation flowed. He found her company anything but tedious. She could cover a vast array of topics knowledgeably. He asked her questions, seeking her opinion on many matters.

"Have you settled into your chambers? Is everything to your liking?" he asked.

"Yes. Tis more than adequate. The solar is remarkable. I thank you," she replied.

"There is no need to thank me. You are mistress here, tis your place as well. I would see that you are comfortable." He paused for a moment, then took a deep breath. "I must return to the Highlands tomorrow. I will be away for some time. I have set aside money for monthly expenses. There is a good allowance for household needs and your funds for clothes and whatever..." He cleared his throat when he thought about her undergarments. "Whatever else you might need."

"Can I spend the money on whatever I want?" Clarissa asked.

"Aye, whatever you want. There are one hundred *seats* each month."

Clarissa was shocked when she heard the amount.

"What? Tis not enough? How much would you prefer?" Dalziel hoped she would not drain his coffers with demands. He knew English women could be over-spenders.

"No, you misunderstand. That is far more generous than anything I've received before. Tis more than enough. I did not expect it."

"You are my wife. I will provide for you."

"How long will you be gone?" she asked.

"A few weeks at the most," he replied.

Clarissa felt disappointed. She enjoyed their straightforward conversation. She would miss him, but he no doubt had many friends and female acquaintances to see.

Chapter 4–When the Wolf's Away

Five weeks later, Finch's Tavern, Bamburgh

The tavern was full of revelers from the usual crowd gathered around the card table and at its center sat the lady of Stanhope. A dram of whisky on the side playing cards.

This was Clarissa's 'safe place' where she felt most at home among the local cottagers and villeins. They, in turn, protected her privacy. Despite her recent rise in status, the patrons treated her as one of their own.

"I raise you five, you crooked nosed knave," Clarissa said whilst downing a cup of ale in her stride.

"You extend yourself too far, me lady, but I'll wager ye seven for a peek at your glorious tits," Bailey, her opposition, taunted.

Clarissa rarely lost at the gaming table. She had the innate ability to count and remember every card passed in a deck. To keep her focus, she rarely drank to excess, but for appearance's sake, she often feigned inebriation.

Her opponent made an error and Clarissa closed in for the kill.

"Poor Bailey, these tits you shall never see." She groped her breasts, then threw down a winning hand.

Bailey cursed, and the whole tavern erupted with cheers. He grumbled, having just lost another twenty yards of his finest linen to Clarissa.

"Damn, you play a mean game."

"That I do you, lecherous churl, but in good faith, I'll pay for this round." Clarissa winked.

She never bet with money, only bartered goods, and most of the goods kept the women and children in garments.

Her absent husband was still oblivious to her activities, and she was happy with that, although his household was another matter entirely.

Mrs. Armstrong and the servants had cottoned on to the fact she spent a great deal at the tavern and *cove*, and rather than reprimand her, they supported her. All except Rupert, who Mrs. Armstrong insisted must never know because, according to her, "The man has a bloody big mouth and will certainly tell the master."

Clarissa did not even want to think about what would happen if Dalziel discovered her double life and that his loyal servants were complicit. But she would cross that bridge if she came to it. In the meantime, she was glad he was away for weeks on end, so she did not have to blatantly lie to his face all the time.

Cedric had still not returned home, but Harmony sent word that he contacted her from a seaport in *Alnwick* and he would return home in due course.

It relieved Clarissa to hear some news at least, and so she patiently awaited his return. She longed to see her brother and missed his mischievous smile. It had always been just the two of them against the world. She hoped he approved of her marital choice.

Clarissa was just thinking about her marriage when the door flew open and Toby shouted, "Ris! Your husband has returned."

"What? But he's not due home for weeks." Clarissa quickly picked up her pace. She paid Marley, the owner, for the round and ran out of the building. "Bailey, I'll be collecting my winnings on the morrow," she yelled over her shoulder.

Clarissa mounted her horse, thanked Toby, then nudged it to a gallop. She bent low and raced across the meadow like the four horsemen of the apocalypse were giving chase. She dared not peer at the road in case she spotted her husband.

Dalziel

DALZIEL HAD BEEN AWAY for several weeks and he was itching to get home. He wondered when he had thought of Stanhope as home. He still hated being in England, but came to accept some things were just the way they were.

Apart from the occasional letter from Mrs. Armstrong and Rupert, he had not heard a word from Clarissa. He wondered what she was doing with herself. More specifically, *who* she was doing things with. His feelings towards his wife bordered on irrational. He thought about her constantly and the longer he was away from her; the obsession grew.

The morning he left for Scotland, Clarissa had wished him well, but there was a hint of eagerness on her part for him to leave. It left him agitated. Women sought him out, they pursued him relentlessly. But not his wife. She could not wait to be rid of him, and that stung.

He was not due home for several weeks, but the time in Scotland left him restless and dissatisfied. He was no closer to finding 'She-wolf,' although the murders had ceased the moment he returned to his Scottish home.

Dalziel thought back to the weeks he had spent away. Not once had he been tempted to take pleasure or comfort from a woman. Lenora, his ex-mistress, had tried several times to re-establish a relationship, yet he could not do it. Despite having a severe case of blue balls. The best he had accomplished was to take matters into his own hand, so to speak, and that was the extent of that. There was a moment of weakness when he was well in his cups at an inn and Lenora appeared. But nothing came of it because even in an intoxicated state, all he wanted was a pair of emerald eyes and flowing auburn hair.

His lips turned into a wry grin just thinking about his wife and her fine eyes that sparkled with amusement. He wondered what it would be like to run his fingers through her hair as he took his pleasure. He interrupted his reverie. This fascination would not do. Clarissa was out of bounds. He needed to attend to estate matters, check-in with

Arrowsmith, and hie back to the Highlands, or he would wind up just like his father.

Dalziel thought about his English mother Minerva. She had twisted his father in knots and abandoned them both for an English nobleman. His father died in battle, nursing a broken heart, pining for a woman unworthy of his love.

Dalziel wondered if Clarissa had a lover. He snarled and clenched his fist at the thought. He stared out the window and something caught his eye. A sight that took his breath away in the far distance. There was a forest nymph galloping across the fields. Glorious hair flowing and riding astride, with scandalously tight breeches revealing shapely thighs. She was magnificent. Then she disappeared.

She reminded him of Clarissa. *No, it could not be her.* His wife was too proper to ride astride in trews.

When Dalziel arrived home, he asked Mr. Bell whether he had seen anyone riding in the area.

"No one's taken any of these horses out today, me lord."

Eventually shrugging it off, Dalziel strode into the house in search of the woman who plagued his thoughts daily.

A Proper Lady

CLARISSA MADE IT TO the back door just in time. She was anxious and out of breath.

Her greatest fear of discovery was that Dalziel would stop her from working for the *Cause* if he found out, and that was something she could not risk. Women and children depended on her, and secrecy was the key to their survival. Most of the women had suffered at the hands of titled wealthy men who assumed it was their right to treat women as they pleased. While Clarissa felt Dalziel was not one of those men, she did not know him enough to trust that he would not insist they returned the women to their husbands or protectors.

Just as she was sneaking through the servant's entrance, Mrs. Armstrong appeared.

"Mistress, come quickly," she said.

They rushed past the library and to a spare chamber below. Mrs. Armstrong opened the chamber door and retrieved a kirtle from a chest. Finola, a maid, came flying through the door seconds later and started helping Clarissa change out of her trews and shirt.

"Why do you all keep helping me?" Clarissa asked, genuinely curious.

"Do ye ken Sally Greene?" Mrs. Armstrong asked.

Clarissa nodded. Sally was a woman she and Cedric had rescued from Goldie's brothel a year earlier. "Yes."

"She is my niece," Mrs. Armstrong replied. "She was never the same after what they did." Mrs. Armstrong paused, as if choking back tears. "I kenned twas your *cause* that got her out of that hellhole and you have my eternal gratitude. If you need to do what you do in secret, then we will not tell."

Finola added, "There are many Sally Greenes out there, Mistress, and no one cares for them, but you do, and we need to protect each other."

Clarissa felt overwhelmed with emotion. They say it takes a village to raise a child. She had proof before her it also takes a village to protect a woman. With their help, Clarissa had just enough time to freshen up and change into a morning dress. Her hair was refastened, and she resembled a proper lady as she made her way to the main entrance just in time to greet her husband.

"Husband? You have returned early. Tis a lovely surprise to see you." She smiled at Dalziel, genuinely pleased to see him.

Dalziel gazed at his wife, and he had to catch his breath. *Glory be, she was a welcome sight.*

"Hello, Ris, I am happy to be home," he replied, and meant it. He kissed her on the cheek. "Just out of curiosity, have you been out riding today?" he asked.

"Yes, but earlier today. I have since been perusing the books," she replied. Theoretically, it was not a lie. Two minutes ago, was considered earlier, and she glimpsed the books as she ran past the study.

Dalziel eyed her up and down and then recollected himself. He tried to reconcile the nymph in the meadow and the woman before him and concluded they could not be the same person.

Clarissa wished not for the first time that there were no secrets between them. She wished she could ask him all the things she eagerly wanted to know but refrained because they vowed to live separate lives. She wondered who Dalziel was spending his nights with. *Did he have a string of mistresses in Scotland?* The jealousy she felt towards these unknown women was unwelcome. She said little and restricted her comments to the weather and local village news.

They passed the day mostly in companionable silence, although Dalziel rarely left her side. When Clarissa sought a reprieve in the library, Dalziel found a book to read and joined her on the settee. If she retreated to her solar, he followed with paperwork, then sat nearby reviewing accounts. When the dinner bell chimed, he escorted her from her bed chamber, and instead of sitting at the head of the table on the opposite end; he repositioned the setting and sat beside her.

At one point, an errant ringlet escaped from her coiffured bun. Dalziel tucked it behind her ear, brushing his fingers across her cheek, and trailed them down her nape.

She shivered with the sensation of it but remained focused on her food lest she choke on her meal.

Dalziel could not help himself. The need to touch his wife overrode all sense of respectability. He had never wanted a woman so much in his life and to have her under his roof while she was out of bounds was torture. He knew she was not unaffected by his presence either, if her shallow breathing was any indication.

That night, as he lay alone in his enormous bed staring up at the ceiling, his thoughts kept returning to his wife. He wondered what she would think if he crossed the threshold that separated their rooms. He stared at the adjoining door, willing it to open of its own volition so he would have an excuse to walk through and damn the consequences. Eventually, he fell asleep, disappointed.

Clarissa tossed and turned on her bed. After supper, they had parted company, and ever since, she felt hot and bothered. As if she needed release, but she knew not from what. She stared at the adjoining door, wondering what her husband was doing. *Was he asleep, naked? What would happen if she walked through that adjoining door and found out for herself?* She let out a muffled scream into her pillow, feeling frustrated and out of sorts.

THAT NEXT MORNING DALZIEL was going over accounts with Rupert when one particular accounting about Clarissa's pin money had Rupert questioning if something was amiss.

"Is she spending the money at all?" Dalziel asked.

"She uses most of it except for savings."

"Then what seems to be the problem?"

"I have observed she does not have many new dresses," Rupert replied.

"So?"

"But there are large bills from the seamstress."

"Then where do all the dresses go?" Dalziel asked.

"I believe she sends them elsewhere or perhaps gives them away."

"Does she purchase anything for herself?"

"Nothing more than undergarments," Rupert replied.

Dalziel felt instantly aroused, thinking of his wife's undergarments, then stopped before his errant thoughts became too salacious. He would monitor her purchases.

Mr. Bell knocked on the door and delivered a missive from King Macbeth. Dalziel gritted his teeth in frustration. It was an urgent summons to Macbeth's Castle in Dunsinane. There was some trouble brewing with Norsemen.

It annoyed Dalziel he could not spend more time with his wife, but a summons from his king was a summons he could not ignore. He left immediately without saying goodbye, as Clarissa was nowhere to be found. He hoped she missed him as much as he knew he would miss her.

Before taking his leave, he stopped in to see Arrowsmith for an update on matters. He also made an unusual personal request.

"Anything you ask, Dalziel, I'll be happy to oblige," Arrowsmith said.

"I want you to keep an eye on my wife. I want to ken her movements when I am away, especially any men she keeps company with and report directly to me."

Arrowsmith raised an eyebrow in question, then agreed. "Aye, I'll keep a close eye on her."

"Thank you. I'd appreciate it if you did not tell any of my household."

"Is everything all right?" Arrowsmith asked.

"Aye, I just want to ken more about my wife, and tis difficult when I have to spend so much time away," Dalziel replied.

"But is that not what you wanted?"

"At first, I did. But now I'm not so sure."

There was silence between them before Arrowsmith said, "I will do as you ask, but Dalziel, a warning. Dinnae let a woman turn your head. That way lies ruin."

CLARISSA RETURNED HOME that night and asked about Dalziel. It disappointed her to discover he had returned to Scotland without saying goodbye. She felt a little depressed. She had been looking forward to spending another evening together. It was an obvious reminder she meant nothing more to him than a temporary wife. She resolved to build sturdier walls around her heart.

Macbeth's Castle, Dunsinane Scotland

DALZIEL FOUND IT DIFFICULT to concentrate on the task at hand. It was the first time something had distracted him from an assignment. Instead of focusing on the multiple threats facing his king, he wondered what Clarissa was doing. *Maybe he should write her a letter.*

"Dalziel!"

He came back to the present and realized the King of Scotland, Macbeth *mac Findlaích*, and his retinue were awaiting Dalziel's answer to a question he had missed.

"Tis sorry I am, Your Majesty. I was trying to work out a plan in my head."

"Hmm... tis not like ye to be so distracted, Dalziel. Is everything all right in Northumbria?" Macbeth asked.

"Aye, tis fine. All is fine," he replied, more to himself.

Macbeth seemed skeptical but continued the meeting. When it was over and the men had dispersed, Macbeth requested Dalziel remain behind for a private talk.

"We have a problem, Dalziel."

"I ken it. I am sorry for my distraction Your Majesty, I promise it willna happen—"

"Tis nothing to do with that. This is entirely a different matter," Macbeth said.

"What is it?" Dalziel appeared confused.

"Lenora."

He stiffened. "What about her?"

"Is she still your current mistress?"

"No, I have not seen her in months. Why?"

"Then mayhap you need to tell her that before she gets out of hand. She places my kingdom at risk with her loose tongue."

Dalziel had worked closely with Macbeth for several years to know this was not a suggestion, but a command. Which meant Lenora had overstepped enough to concern Macbeth. This did not surprise Dalziel. It was a myriad of reasons he ended their arrangement. Lenora was an opportunist, always seeking leverage to advance her position.

Despite his friendly demeanor and affable appearance, Macbeth was a shrewd strategist and vicious warrior with a reputation for turning battlefields red with blood. The reason they called him 'The Red King.' He also controlled an intricate web of spies spread throughout several kingdoms, stretching all the way to Rome. Macbeth wielded a tightly woven tapestry of influence and political power. Any person perceived to be a threat received a warning, the second warning came as death. Macbeth's message was clear: Lenora was about to receive her only warning.

"I will see to it. You have my word," Dalziel replied.

Glencoe, Highlands, Scotland - Cutting Ties

DALZIEL SAT ACROSS from Lenora in her Drawing Room. She was his ex-mistress. Their relationship ended amicably months ago. But word was, she was making it known they were still together to garner favor within the Scottish court. Such falsehoods affected Dalziel's work and reputation, and he needed to put an end to it.

Dalziel studied Lenora as she sat primping. She was a voluptuous woman with a preference for garments that bared a lot of flesh. Her movements were also fluid and sensual. She had been trained by the best courtesans and commanded an exorbitant fee for her services. He knew firsthand she was experienced in bed sport and Sybaritic pleasures. For a man like him who led a hard life of violence and secrecy, she had satisfied his physical needs and filled a void of intimacy others could not provide. Her allure lay in her hedonistic tendencies.

But in the lead up to him ending things, she had become more possessive and demanding of his time. Their boundaries had always been clearly defined, but she pushed for a relationship that had already run its course. Dalziel needed a clean slate so he could carry out his duty to the King.

"We need to talk, Nora."

"I kenned you would come back to me, darling, twas only a matter of time before you missed me," she said.

"I have not come back, Nora. I request you accept our arrangement is over and not spread rumors to the contrary."

"I refuse to believe that." She pouted.

"I have taken my seat in Northumbria, and I'll be there for some time. Tis over, this is not just from me, Nora, but also a warning from King Macbeth. Tread carefully."

Lenora paled slightly at the mention of Macbeth, then whined, "Why must we end things? I could easily move to Northumbria with you and keep you company on those frosty nights."

"I am married now," he replied.

She was stunned and demanded, "Who is she?"

"She is English."

"You married a *Sassenach* over me?" Lenora screeched.

"Aye, I did. But I never offered you marriage, Nora. You kenned that from the beginning. Heed my words well. Our arrangement is well and truly over."

The Problem

DALZIEL WAS BACK IN Dunsinane, sitting in Macbeth's private study going over several matters with his king.

"Is it done?" Macbeth asked.

"Aye. Lenora will not be a problem anymore."

"Good. Now, tell me, how does your new marriage fare. Clarissa Harcourt, is it?"

"It bodes well. Although I am much away from home to warrant any sort of deep connection between us. I have been focused on Earl Siward."

Macbeth took a deep breath then said, "That is what I want to talk to you about. I have since received further news from my sources."

"What do they report?"

"Twould appear there is a group of powerful men in Northumbria who are close to Siward. Arrowsmith has been keeping vigil over their movements," Macbeth replied.

"What are their names?" Dalziel asked.

"Chamberlain, Lancet, and Davenport. Do you ken them?"

"No."

"My sources in the South, tell me James Davenport is the ringleader. Word is he is searching for someone who stole a list of names, that could destroy Siward. I want that list Dalziel and I want to find this person before he does."

"Who is it?"

"His wife," Macbeth replied.

"Do you ken where she might be?" Dalziel asked.

"No, she went into hiding and vanished. Davenport wants her dead and he has several men hunting for her. So, wherever she is, she is in great danger, and whoever is helping her doesna fare much better."

Dalziel was shocked. *What kind of man killed his wife?*

"I will send out some of my men to search," Dalziel said. "What is her name?" he asked.

"Elspeth Davenport," Macbeth replied.

Chapter 5 - Homecoming

1044 MacGregor Land, Glenorchy

Dalziel

Dalziel was attending May Day celebrations with his family and his clan. He was longing to return to Northumbria but matters in Scotland had kept him away longer than expected.

While he loved being with his brothers and their families, he felt restless. Beiste and Brodie had settled down with two women Dalziel admired and respected. They now had bairns running around, causing mischief. He would die to protect the love his brothers had found, but that only left a hollow ache in his chest. A yearning for something similar.

He often wondered how Clarissa was faring. Arrowsmith had sent several updates on her movements, but none of which caused Dalziel concern.

It had been two months since he had last seen her and although everyone at the estate sent him letters; he had yet to receive a single word from her. He could not comprehend why it bothered him so much when it was, he who had made it clear they were to lead separate lives. But one would *think* a wife would at least send her husband some type of correspondence. Even if it was to talk about the bloody weather.

A messenger interrupted him with a missive from Arrowsmith. Dalziel studied the parchment and clenched his jaw when he read, "Lady Clarissa seen in the company of an unknown French man."

What had he told her about taking lovers? Dalziel saw red. This was the final straw. Something snapped inside, and all the pent-up frustration bubbled to the surface. It did not help that he had forgone sexual relations since meeting his damned wife, not even to take the edge off when his role was demanding.

"What is it?" Beiste asked, carrying his two-month-old son, Dalziel Brodie MacGregor.

"I need to leave now. There is trouble brewing at my estate in *Anglia*."

"What kind of trouble? Brodie piped in, holding his sleeping daughter, Izara.

"Tis my wife," Dalziel replied.

They all stared in surprise. "You have a wife?"

"Aye, and I need to remind her who she belongs to," Dalziel growled.

Stanhope Estate, Bamburgh, Northumbria

DALZIEL ARRIVED CLOSE to midnight. He had ridden hard through thundering rain all the way from Scotland with minimal rest stops.

He arrived unannounced. The element of surprise was always a good way to discover what was really afoot. The way the servants scurried around like frightened mice at his appearance made him glad he did.

He stormed inside the main foyer and was accosted by Mr. Bell and Mrs. Armstrong.

"Me lord! We were not expecting you tonight. Is everything all right?" Mrs. Armstrong asked as Mr. Bell took his sodden coat and handed him a towel to dry his hair.

"Aye, I am sorry I did not send word, but some urgent business had me returning early. Where is Lady Clarissa?" Dalziel asked calmly.

"She is..." Mr. Bell glanced at Mrs. Armstrong. They appeared nervous.

"Not in," Mrs. Armstrong replied.

"What do you mean she is not in? Tis almost midnight?" Dalziel said.

He turned to Mr. Bell, awaiting a response. He saw servants in the background hovering.

"Lady Clarissa is attending a gathering," Mr. Bell replied.

"Which one? I ken no such event happening tonight," Dalziel asked, sounding calm, although inside he was feeling the opposite.

Dalziel could see the servants were uncomfortable. But he had done his research and no assembly or events were happening within the shire, that would warrant his wife being out in this inclement weather.

Mr. Bell cast a nervous glance at Mrs. Armstrong, who subtly shrugged her shoulders. At a loss for words.

Dalziel knew they were hiding something, even the maids were complicit. If he found out his wife was cuckolding him, he would lose his mind. Without another word, he walked up the flight of stairs and began opening every single door, thinking he might find Clarissa with a lover.

The more he searched, the angrier he became. He never allowed anger or any emotion to dictate his behavior until now. Dalziel was standing on the landing above the entrance when the main doors opened, and a figure came marching in with confident strides.

Then he heard her voice. Dalziel stilled and peered down at the grand entranceway.

"Bugger me, Cecil," she said to Mr. Bell, taking off her coat. "The weather is cold out. Damn near froze my tits off. But look..." She fished something out of her pocket and gave it to Mrs. Armstrong. "I won it back. All right... I admit I cheated, but they stole it, so in this case, two wrongs make a right."

Dalziel stared at the woman in the moon's light, and it was as if he was staring down at a... stranger. She had his wife's voice, but that was where the resemblance ended. Underneath the coat, she wore trews, a shirt, a cap, and flat boots. Anyone peering from afar would think she was a lad.

A riot of auburn hair spilled out when she pulled the cap off. She was wet, and her clothes clung to every aspect of her body. She kept talking, wringing out her hair as the servants handed her towels. All subtly gesturing for Clarissa to be quiet.

He wondered who this strange woman was who could garner the loyalty of his staff? What was this manner of dress and speech? This was not the proper lady he had married. That female was a paragon of propriety and boring pursuits and rarely spoke a crass word... but this... this woman was something else entirely.

Mr. Bell cleared his throat, trying to give Clarissa warning signals, but she carried on oblivious. "Oh, before I forget, I've sent word that no one heads to the *cove* tonight. Tis especially dangerous where they've stored the—."

"Mistress! We have company," Mrs. Armstrong practically scream-shouted over her.

Clarissa stopped drying her hair and asked, "At this hour? Who is it?"

Dalziel moved down the staircase, trying to keep his possessive fury in check. She must have sensed his approach, because she spun around in shock and gasped when she saw him.

Dalziel took in her lush, wet figure and her flushed face and stalked towards her. The wolf within him unleashed with a feral need to claim what was rightfully his. *What had always been his!* When he was standing directly in front of her, he stared into her emerald eyes and in a lethal voice said, "Hello, Wife! Where the hell have you been?"

Show Down

CLARISSA FELT BREATHLESS. It had been so long since she had seen Dalziel; she had almost forgotten the raw, masculine energy he exuded. Right now, he was like an untethered wild beast.

She scrambled to think of something to say, any story, but like a startled deer she replied, "I was just searching for…"

"Dragons?" Dalziel said sarcastically.

"Maybe?" She twisted the towel she held in her hand and bit her lip with uncertainty.

Dalziel stared at her succulent mouth and snarled, "Wrong answer!"

He bent low to her waist and hefted her over his shoulder, then stormed up the stairs.

"No one is to disturb us, and I will deal with you all later," he shouted at his recalcitrant staff.

"Do not hurt her. Tis not her fault about the brothel," Mr. Bell beseeched him and followed up the stairs.

Mrs. Armstrong ran ahead of them and blocked the door to Dalziel's chamber. "My lord, ye will not harm her no matter what you find out about her nighttime activities."

"What brothel? What nighttime activities?" Dalziel roared, thinking this affair with a French man must be worse than he suspected.

"Mrs. Armstrong, Cecil, you are not helping!" Clarissa hissed, while hanging upside down.

"I have never harmed a woman, Mrs. Armstrong, but I will get to the truth. Now move," Dalziel demanded.

The staff relented and, with that, Dalziel stormed into his bed chambers, slammed, and locked the door. Then he tossed Clarissa onto the bed.

She tried to scramble away, but he grabbed her ankles and dragged her back. "So, help me Wife, if you dinnae start talking soon, I am going to tie you to my bed for a week." His tone was threatening.

Dalziel was panting. His clothes were wet and so were hers from the storm.

Clarissa lay on her back, propped up on her elbows, and they stared one another down.

The more Dalziel glared at his wife, the more he wanted her. He wanted her with a ferocious need he thought he would combust.

"What is his name?" he asked.

"Who?"

"The French man."

"You mean Pierre or Jean-Luc?"

"There are two?" he roared.

Clarissa sat up. "Yes." She was confused.

Dalziel turned away from her and slammed his fist into the wooden door. The wood splintered.

"What is the matter with you?" she shouted at him and clambered off the bed. She grabbed his fist, which was bleeding. "Why are you so angry?" She found a cloth and began wiping the blood.

"You have two French lovers, and you ask me why I'm angry?" He fumed.

"Lovers? Are you daft? They're my cousins."

He halted. "Cousins? You have French cousins?"

"Aye, on my mother's side."

"You are part French?"

"*Oui.*"

Dalziel stilled. *How did he not know this about her?*

Clarissa kept examining his knuckle and wiping the blood. "You're lucky you did not break your bones, you foolish man." She glowered. "It will be sore for a few days and serves you right if it turns out to be broken. Now sit down," she ordered.

Having all the righteous indignation knocked out of him, Dalziel slumped into the chair while she fussed over him. Now and then she shivered but kept moving.

Ire abated; Dalziel gazed at his wife as she tended to his grazed knuckle. An errant curl blocked his view of her face as she bent to place a cold cloth on his hand. He reached out and tucked it back behind her ear.

"Where were you tonight? Please dinnae lie to me." His voice was a plea.

Clarissa sighed, "I was at Finch's Tavern. There is a game of cards there. I go sometimes to place wagers and find information."

"About what?"

"My brother, Cedric. He has been missing for months now and I have been trying to find him."

"And so, you wear these clothes to go to the tavern?"

"Yes, tis safer to blend in if people think I am a man."

"Do you do this regularly, these nighttime activities?"

She hesitated, then replied, "Yes."

"And the gaming?"

"Only if I am certain I can win."

"And how do you ken that?"

She shivered again. "I have a talent for remembering cards, and I choose my opponents wisely."

Dalziel blinked as if he were seeing someone else entirely. Begrudgingly, he was impressed.

"Did you win anything?"

"Yes, a pearl necklace stolen from Mrs. Armstrong. I cheated a little. I made sure the thief was drunk before I wagered for it." She peered up at him guiltily.

"And did you find any information about your brother?"

"Only that he ventured to *Dalmally* in Scotland several weeks ago." She finished cleaning his wound.

Dalziel recalled the body at *Dalmally*. He wondered if they were connected. A feeling of dread came over him, but he shook it off. He made a mental note to follow up regarding the identity of the man in the ditch. "I will help you search for your brother."

Clarissa stared at him as if he hung the moon and stars in the sky. In astonishment. "You will?"

"Aye."

"Thank you." She held back tears. It had been difficult trying to care for the women and children and search for Cedric. This was welcome news.

Dalziel gazed at Clarissa and noticed she was shivering. Then he realized neither one of them had changed out of their wet clothes.

"Blast it. Why didn't you tell me you're freezing?" he said.

He opened the door to request some warm water when Mrs. Armstrong and a team of servants carried in two tubs and buckets of boiling water.

"Tis about time. We've had the water heating for both of you."

Clarissa's teeth were chattering, and Dalziel cursed himself for not seeing to her first.

When the servants left, he began removing her clothes and shoes. Her lips were turning blue, and her fingers were ice cold. It was his fault he had left her talking for so long.

She tried to slap his hands away, but he ignored her.

"What are ye doing?" She shivered again.

"I am stripping you bare and placing you in a hot bath. What do you think I am doing?"

Despite her protests, he removed her shirt. She placed her arms across her chest to cover her breasts from view.

Dalziel gritted his teeth and forced himself to think of anything else but the luscious, naked woman in front of him. He was not a brute; he would not ravish his wife... *yet*.

He removed the rest of her clothing, picked her up, ignoring her long shapely legs and rounded bottom, and placed her in the bath.

She moaned in pleasure as the heated water enveloped her as she sank deeper.

"That's it, love, you need to get warm. It will not do to catch an ague."

Dalziel walked to the fireplace, added more wood and boiled more water, then returned with a cloth.

"What's that for?"

"I'm going to help bathe you. Then get you warm so you can get into bed."

She just nodded as her teeth kept chattering. Too cold to argue anymore. "What about you?" she asked.

"I'll take my bath afterward."

When her bath was complete, she felt warmer and suddenly exhausted.

"Here, drink this. It will help with the cold," Dalziel said.

Clarissa drank the whiskey Dalziel held out for her and it heated her blood. When she stood to get out of the tub, Dalziel did not hesitate. He wrapped a cloth around her and carried her to the chair by the fire. He then helped her get dry.

It was hell touching his wife so intimately, especially with all her soft curves. Dalziel was pleased to see she had filled out some more, which meant she was eating well. He averted his eyes from her perfectly rounded breasts and rose-colored nipples and the juncture between her thighs. She was blushing enough already without him ogling her. His primary focus was on keeping her warm.

Ten minutes later, Clarissa wore a shift and thick woolen plaid around her while Dalziel towel-dried her hair.

"Thank you, Husband," she whispered.

"Tis my pleasure, Sweeting," he replied.

When she was settled, Dalziel stripped out of his wet clothes. He walked naked to the fire to retrieve the pot of scalding water and poured it in his tub to warm the tepid water. He got in and bathed quickly.

Clarissa tried to turn away, but the sight of her naked husband did strange things to her insides and did far more to heat her flesh than the warm bath.

It was strange they had been married several months, yet this was the most intimate they had ever been. It felt natural to be in his chambers with him like this.

She could hear the water splashing as Dalziel scrubbed himself clean. Then he stood, got out, and dried himself in front of the fire. No inhibitions at all.

Clarissa surreptitiously studied his physique and found nothing wanting. She blushed at the sight of his firm thighs and his semi aroused phallus. She spun away. When next she saw her husband, he had wrapped a woolen plaid around his waist and over his shoulder. He was perfection.

Clarissa rose to return to her room and let him rest.

"Where are you going?" he asked.

"To... to my own chambers," she stammered.

"It would be warmer if we shared my bed," Dalziel replied. "I dinnae want you catching a fever."

She seemed undecided.

"I'll not ravish you, Sweeting."

She agreed, then climbed into his bed. Dalziel got in beside her and drew the surrounding covers. He moved in closer so Clarissa could rest her head against his chest. She burrowed deep, and he kissed her forehead.

"Go to sleep, Love, we have much to discuss in the morning."

Clarissa was too tired to wonder what they had to discuss. It had been an arduous night, and she just wanted to sleep. It had been so long since she felt protected and warm. The worries of the past few months melted away. She closed her eyes and drifted off almost immediately, snuggled safely against her warm Highlander.

Dalziel held Clarissa in his arms, and he knew then everything had changed. The intimacy they had just shared, he had never experienced with any woman before. For the first time in months, maybe even years, his restless soul felt at peace. Come the morning, things were going to change between them. He would draw out all her secrets because he wanted a true marriage.

DALZIEL WOKE AT PRE-dawn, feeling content. He felt a weight on his chest and glimpsed down to see Clarissa resting there, one arm across his stomach and one thigh was thrown over his leg. She was fast asleep and curled against him. He smiled as he caressed her back. She looked so peaceful. He kissed her forehead, and she snuggled closer.

Dalziel was no saint. He had his fair share of lovers, but they never slept the night in his bed. It was his golden rule. He never stayed a full night cuddling with a woman. It was too intimate and left him vulnerable. But waking up beside Clarissa felt *right*. Having her in his bed was something he wanted to experience more of. He smiled at the warmth that was thawing his icy heart. He opened himself to the wonder of allowing the feeling to take root.

He wondered if this was what Beiste and Brodie felt about their wives? If so, it would explain their irrational behavior towards Amelia and Zala. For the first time, Dalziel understood what his brothers went through daily, and he felt real empathy towards them.

The first matter of business in the morning was to start over. Dalziel needed trust established between them. He also wanted to consummate their marriage because he had a burning desire to know Clarissa in all ways. His mind made up, his plan set out, he drifted back to sleep.

Three hours later Dalziel awoke frustrated because his wife was no longer in his bed.

Chapter 6—A Marriage in Truth

Dalziel found Clarissa in her solar writing letters.

He stood in the doorway, mesmerized by her countenance, and thinking how fortunate he was to have found her. "Morning, Love," he greeted.

Clarissa glanced up from her writing and blushed. "Morning, Husband."

"You left our bed before I could do this." Dalziel crossed the distance between them, leaned down, and brushed a kiss over her lips. Then he stood to leave.

But Clarissa did something unexpected. She rose from her chair, went up on tiptoes, and gifted him with a lingering kiss. Dalziel wrapped his arms around her, pulled out the pins, keeping her hair bound, and ran his fingers through the abundant curls. He deepened the kiss and groaned. She tasted sweet and innocent, and her breath smelled of mint. His blood was on fire. He craved her caress and knew from her timid gestures she was an innocent. Dalziel felt humbled knowing that he alone would claim her. He made a silent vow that he would bring her unimaginable pleasure, and he would love and protect her.

When they came up for air, they were panting, and their lips were inches apart. Dalziel whispered, "I want things to change between us?"

"How so?" Clarissa appeared dazed and confused.

"I want a true marriage. I want you in my bed every night. Do you want the same thing?"

Clarissa peered into her husband's eyes and saw a combination of desire and vulnerability. He was nervous about her response. Afraid of rejection, yet brave enough to take a chance.

"I want you too," she replied.

Dalziel beamed and breathed a sigh of relief. "Then we should spend more time together to ken one another better."

She nodded. Wondering if she was prepared to tell him everything about herself.

"Why dinnae we start now? Come, Wife, let's spend today talking and mayhap tonight we can do *other* things." He winked at her, and Clarissa just laughed.

They spent the rest of the day in each other's company, sharing some information about themselves. But not all. Neither one prepared to divulge all their secrets so soon.

In the evening, Dalziel was called away to meet Arrowsmith about urgent matters.

The Three Lords

THAT EVENING, DALZIEL sat in Arrowsmith's study, while they exchanged information.

"All the lies I have spread have come to naught, which leads me to believe the murderer is not in our homes or the usual haunts," Arrowsmith said.

Dalziel agreed. "Aye, I too uncovered nothing while I was in Scotland."

Arrowsmith opened a desk drawer and pulled out some parchments. "I have kept a close eye on Chamberlain, Lancet, and Davenport. They are all members of the peerage and run a gaming establishment for titled wealthy gentlemen. Fittingly called *The Three Lords*."

"How does one gain entry into this wealthy establishment?" Dalziel asked.

"Tis by invite-only," Arrowsmith replied, then picked up two notes.

"What are those?"

"Our invitations." He smirked. "My clerk secured them for us. I say we see what this establishment is about."

Dalziel sniggered. "Aye, ready when you are."

It did not take long for Dalziel and Arrowsmith to realize they had entered a den of iniquity. 'The Three Lords' was a lurid display of hedonism and debauchery. It was a gaudy place filled with members of the peerage who gorged themselves on every vice imaginable beyond the purview of polite society. Part brothel, part gaming, hell, and entirely sinful.

However, Dalziel and Arrowsmith extracted more information in that one venue than in all their weeks of searching.

One thing was clear to Dalziel, the three lords were up to their necks in sinister dealings.

Davenport had taken a special liking to Dalziel, and when he was in his cups, he loosened his tongue, divulging far more than was wise for a man of his ilk.

Dalziel hated him on sight. He thought him arrogant and crass. But it was the way Davenport treated the women in the establishment which raised his ire. Davenport viewed them as objects to slake his lust and predilection for violence. Several of the light skirts sported bruises from his rough handling.

Dalziel had come across men like Davenport before. Their arrogance unchecked often led to their demise. If there was one thing Dalziel learned from being the king's assassin, it was that power was an ever-swinging pendulum. Whoever held it became the target for those who coveted it. For now, Davenport was the ruler of his domain, but he was a fool, oblivious to the hatred directed at him from his peers and the lower classes. Dalziel knew it was only a matter of time before they usurped his position, and he doubted the transition of power would be a peaceful one.

When Dalziel returned home, he washed the moral filth from his body, then went in search of his wife. She was asleep in her bedchamber. He settled in beside her and breathed in her sweet, clean scent.

Dream Lover

CLARISSA OPENED HER eyes. She felt exhausted and weary. The night sky had turned grey and there was a chill in the air, yet she felt warm. She pressed her body closer to the heat source and felt something weigh her down. It was Dalziel's arm encircling her and his thigh entangled with hers.

"Dalziel? What are you doing here?" she asked.

"I told you I want a proper marriage." He brushed a kiss across her lips. "Do you ken what I need, love?"

Clarissa nodded.

"Are you ready to be my wife?"

"I... I have never done this before. I am afraid I may not be good at it."

Dalziel wanted to shout to the rafters, *Mine!* "You dinnae have to worry, love, just trust me to take care of you."

"Is this a dream?" Clarissa asked.

"Would a dream lover do this?" He drew her chemise down and brushed his knuckles against her bare breast. He bent forward and laved her nipple with his tongue before suckling the stiffened peak.

Clarissa moaned and instinctively moved closer.

Dalziel fought to maintain control. He had been hard for months, but he would make this good for her. Her first time was a *gift*, and he would rush nothing. She deserved to feel ecstasy and pleasure.

He tore her chemise, so her entire body was accessible to his touch.

"Would a dream lover do this?" He bent and laved the other nipple into a stiffened peak while his hands caressed her heated flesh.

Clarissa moaned and held his head in place, running her fingers through his hair.

He slowly kissed a path up her neck and whispered in her ear, "I am not a dream and tis time." Dalziel kissed her again, then thrust his tongue in her mouth. She responded on instinct, and it undid him. The kiss turned into more and before long, they were both naked while Dalziel covered her body with his own.

Dalziel licked a path to her belly button. He imagined someday a child of his growing there and he wanted to beat his chest like a cave dweller. He moved lower, making his way to the heart of her. When he arrived at the juncture between her thighs, he spread her legs apart, peering at her molten core.

Clarissa blushed with embarrassment. "What are you doing down there?"

"I need to prepare you to take me, love. Trust me, you will love my methods."

Dalziel saw her hooded pearl engorged and fully aroused. He bent forward and swirled his tongue around her nub, then he suckled hard, intermittently sweeping his scorching tongue across her heated flesh.

Clarissa almost came off the bed when she felt the pressure on her most intimate part. Her eyes rolled to the back of her head. She clutched the sheets and shuddered at the intensity of the pleasure she was experiencing.

Dalziel felt his wife's core grow slick as he maintained pressure. He knew she was ready to take him when her body became rigid as she moaned her orgasm. Dalziel could not wait any longer. His length wept with anticipation. He leisurely moved up her body and cradled his hips between her thighs. Clarissa languidly opened her eyes in astonishment. Dalziel now hovered above her, arms braced on either side, holding his weight off her.

"Do it, love," he rasped.

Clarissa instinctively knew what he meant, as she could feel his hard length nudging her entrance. She reached down and gently placed him at her center.

"Now place your hands around my waist." He groaned.

She did.

He began gliding his length against her, and Clarissa gasped at the sensation.

"I'm sorry, love, the first time will hurt, but it will get better, I promise."

She gazed up at him with complete trust.

Dalziel was a riot of emotions. His wife was a sensory overload of torrid pleasure. She felt exquisite. He stroked himself against her, then pushed inside.

She moaned, and her breathing became shallow. Dalziel withdrew, then repeated the process, gaining more access each time until he felt a barrier. He gloried, knowing that he was her first, that no man had entered beyond this point. He focused on making this moment memorable for her. Dalziel bent his head lower and suckled her nipple. Clarissa became increasingly wetter. Then, in one hard thrust, he surged forward and claimed her as his own.

Clarissa tensed. He was so large she thought the invasion would split her in two. She tried to push him away. But he gentled her. "Calm love. Breathe slowly."

When she relaxed, the pain subsided, replaced by a unique feeling, an insatiable need. Only then did Dalziel move. He pumped his length slowly, and she rose to meet his thrusts. The crescendo was building again. They were both panting. Dalziel picked up his pace as his thrusts became harder. He was grunting with pleasure, which aroused Clarissa even more. She felt invincible that she could garner such passions from her husband. She responded in kind as they moved as one. Their movements became desperate, disjointed as Dalziel pounded into her with force. That familiar feeling returned; she was flying towards ecstasy.

"Canna last much longer, Love, I need you to come with me," Dalziel murmured desperate words of encouragement in her ear.

He kneaded her center with his thumb; it was the pressure needed to take her over the edge. Clarissa detonated. She moaned in pleasure as her channel contracted, sheathing him like a glove. Dalziel shouted his climax as his body jerked several times, filling her with his essence. When he was spent, he collapsed on top of her, then shifted her to his side.

They spent several moments catching their breath, kissing and caressing one another.

"You're mine, Ris." He kissed the tip of her nose. "Do you ken it?"

She nodded.

"No one touches you but me," he growled.

Clarissa planted a kiss on his chest and whispered, "No one but you."

Dalziel got out of bed, then returned a second later with a warm cloth and before Clarissa could protest; he wiped away the evidence of their coupling from between her thighs. He cleaned himself and discarded the cloth. Then got back in beside her. Dalziel tugged her body against his and said, "Sleep *mo leannan*." – *My sweetheart.*

Clarissa nuzzled closer and did just that.

Dalziel lay awake as his wife slept, and he knew he was never letting her go.

FOR SEVERAL DAYS DALZIEL and Clarissa fell into a comfortable rhythm. At night, they indulged in sensual pleasures as Dalziel taught her scandalous and novel ways to find pleasure and release. During the day, they went their separate ways. Neither one had fully disclosed their secret lives, but as it did not affect their marriage, they carried on as usual.

Dalziel and Arrowsmith continued to frequent *'The Three Lords'*. Neither partook of the services on offer. Dalziel did not need to indulge in hedonistic pleasures when he had a wife at home who satisfied him.

One thing he had learned was of the three men, Davenport, was the most dangerous. He reported directly to Earl Siward of Northumbria. Davenport was also embittered that his wife left him several weeks ago, and he believed she was in hiding with a lover.

Dalziel found it ironic that Davenport called Elspeth *'faithless'* and *'adulterous,'* yet the man kept several mistresses and often partook of the establishment's public orgies. Dalziel would never understand the double standards of English noblemen. However, he remained close to Davenport because he knew eventually, he would find the information he needed for Macbeth.

All Dalziel needed now was to find Elspeth Davenport.

Little did he know two secret worlds were about to collide and the result would end in death.

Chapter 7 – French Connection

It was a warm day when Clarissa visited her home at Driftwood Cottage. She was so excited to see the roof fixed, and the windows repaired. The cottage was freshly painted, and the garden was thriving; the meadows were bursting with life and the sea air did wonders for her soul.

They had restored the large cottage to its former glory, thanks to the pin money she had set aside to make it livable. The larder was stocked, and the vegetable garden also provided food for the *safe house*.

Martin and Ruth now lived there full time, maintaining the premises, and Clarissa provided them with wages for their services. She accepted they would most likely live with her in their dotage, as they had no children of their own and she wanted them to live in comfort.

Pierre and Jean-Luc also found a warm welcome home there whenever they passed through.

She often wondered what would have happened to them all if Dalziel had not intervened and saved her from the brink of starvation. One day, she hoped to repay him for his kindness towards her and her family.

The more she thought about it, the more she realized Dalziel was a good man. He had many secrets, but so did she. Her only regret was that Cedric could not enjoy this new life with them. He was the big brother, the adopted son, the wise cousin who had protected and provided for them all during lean times. Now, when there was abundance and a time of plenty, he was missing out.

"Ris, come join us," Pierre called out from behind the house. She saw they were all gathered in the back, having a picnic. Martin, Ruth, Jean-Luc, and Pierre were outside making the most of the warmer evenings.

Clarissa added her basket of goods to their picnic table, including some wine she brought from the Stanhope cellar.

Jean-Luc immediately poured the homemade wine he was drinking, onto the ground, snatched the wine bottle in Clarissa's basket, and said, *"La vie est trop courte pour boire du mauvais vin."–Life is too short to drink bad wine.*

Clarissa just grinned.

After an enjoyable feast, Ruth and Martin retired back inside while the three cousins walked along the beach. They talked and laughed about everything and nothing, sometimes in English, sometimes in French. All of them worried about Cedric, each hopeful he would return soon. Clarissa was enjoying their time together so much she had forgotten about the assembly she was to attend with Dalziel that night.

Dalziel made his way to Clarissa's cottage. He had never been there before, but Mrs. Armstrong told him that was where she had gone. He heard voices from the back of the house and followed the sound. That was when he saw Clarissa and two men lying on the beach rolling around in laughter. When he came closer, he saw one man, the dark-haired one, had his arm linked with hers. It was an easy natural gesture as if they were close, intimate–*was this a lover?*

Dalziel saw red. He narrowed the distance between them and stormed towards Clarissa. In one swift move, he pulled her out of the man's arms, hauled her off the ground, and secured his arm firmly around her waist. Then, turning to the others, he asked, "What the Hell is going on here?"

Clarissa inhaled a sharp breath, still reeling from the shock of seeing Dalziel and from being held in an iron grip. The moment struck her as ridiculous that her cousins were cursing her husband in French, while Dalziel traded barbs in English.

She giggled. It was funny; the situation was funny. She dared to stare into his eyes and burst out laughing.

"What is so funny?" he glowered. "And who are these scoundrels?"

"Scoundrels? You are the scoundrel!" Pierre spat on the ground.

"They are not scoundrels. These are my cousins, Pierre and Jean-Luc." Clarissa tried to placate Dalziel.

Dalziel stared at Jean-Luc again and remembered him from the dock the night he and Arrowsmith intervened in a brawl. He frowned. "You were at the dock that night," he said.

Dalziel then whipped his head around to Clarissa and said, "That's how you got the bruised cheek. It was you, wasn't it? You're the lad that was fighting down near the brothel!"

Not waiting for an answer, Dalziel glared at her cousins, pointing a finger at their faces. "How the hell could you let her brawl with men at the docks? You imbeciles!" he shouted.

Affronted, Pierre and Jean-Luc started shouting back mostly in expletives, and Clarissa was trying to calm all three of them down, which was difficult when Dalziel kept nudging her to the side.

Eventually, Martin appeared to break it up, and when Dalziel realized Martin was also at the docks that night, he gave Martin a blistering earful. Pierre and Jean-Luc came to Martin's defense, and then there were four grown men yelling at each other down on the beach.

Clarissa argued it was her choice, but none of them listened to her, so she gave up. She marched back up to the house, poured a glass of wine, and started drinking.

It was Ruth who sorted them all out, eventually by yelling at all of them for upsetting Clarissa. "You're family now. So ye best start getting along for the sake of that lass sitting up there drinking alone," Ruth said.

The men were contrite. Dalziel apologized for interrupting their day, and they made their way back to the house. Dalziel was quiet all the way home. From what he gathered from her family; Clarissa was always putting her life in danger. He was going to put a stop to that.

Town Hall, Bamburgh– 'Mother Dearest'

LATER THAT EVENING, Clarissa and Dalziel dressed and attended the town assembly together.

Dalziel and Arrowsmith had been keeping a close eye on Davenport, Lancet, and Chamberlain. This was the only reason Dalziel had agreed to attend the assembly, and he kept Clarissa close. If she moved too far away, he hauled her back.

Clarissa noticed Dalziel never left her side. If he needed to talk to people, he would either drag her with him or leave her with Arrowsmith. It was as if he was subconsciously guarding her. Clarissa had just spotted Harmony and was about to walk over to speak to her when Dalziel jerked her back. His body was tense, and he was furious. He held her hand in a death grip. She followed his gaze and stilled. A woman was walking towards them, and she seemed familiar somehow.

"Son! Oh, how marvelous to see you," she said to Dalziel.

Dalziel's grip on Clarissa's hand tightened. He gritted his teeth and grunted, "*Màthair.*"

Dalziel stared at the woman who birthed him, and his blood ran cold. She was conniving and cunning. She left his father for a wealthy nobleman and abandoned her only son. In a fitting turn of events, the nobleman ran out of money, and Dalziel's English grandfather, disgusted with his daughter's behavior, left everything to Dalziel. She now relied on Dalziel for an annuity, which he provided. But they had no ties beyond fiscal duty.

"Darling, how is your dear Papa?"

"Dead."

She gasped. "I... I am sorry, my dear boy, I did not realize—"

"Aye, he was killed in battle five years ago, still carrying a flame for you."

"Son, I—"

"It has been a lovely chat, Ma. If you dinnae mind, we must be on our way." He made to move around her.

His mother remarked, "And who is this charming creature beside you?" She gave Clarissa a once-over and scrunched up her nose, making it clear she did not approve.

"Tis my wife," Dalziel replied.

"Wife?" His mother was shocked. "But what about Lenora? Surely you did not pass her over for this—"

"Watch what words come out of your mouth," Dalziel replied with venom in his tone.

She backed down. "I just meant that you and Lenora have been so close all these years."

"Lenora and I have no arrangement and she is well aware."

"But she was always your favorite." His mother, Minerva, pouted.

Dalziel could feel Clarissa tense the more his mother spoke. He instinctively pulled her to his side and kept his arm around her waist. It was something most men did not do in public, but he would be damned if he let his mother's vicious tongue hurt his woman.

"Well, speak of the devil... here is Lenora now." His mother feigned surprise.

Dalziel met Lenora's eyes and his body went numb. *What was she doing here?*

Clarissa stared at the goddess standing before them. She had raven black hair and her ample breasts were ready to spill out of her gown. The one emotion Clarissa felt in spades was envy. She was green with it. As a woman, she knew she was facing Dalziel's past lover, someone who had known her husband intimately, and by comparison, Clarissa felt like a rag doll in a pawnshop. The woman was stunning.

"Lenora, what are you doing here?" Dalziel gave her a quelling look.

"Darling, is that any way to speak to your mistress?"

"Former mistress. Again, what are you doing here?"

"I've missed you." She pouted. "Last time you visited, you mentioned you were moving here, so I followed." She shrugged her shoulders.

"Why?" Dalziel raised his brow.

"So, I could do this." Lenora crossed the distance between them and before he could stop her, she nudged Clarissa out of the way, grabbed Dalziel's head, and planted a kiss on his lips.

Dalziel jerked his head out of her hands and stepped back. Then he watched as if in slow motion, red liquid float across the space between them, it suspended in midair for a fraction of a second and then splashed all over Lenora's face. She shrieked and tried to shield herself, but the damage was already done.

Dalziel glanced at his wife. Clarissa's hand was still mid-air, nursing an empty cup.

"Never kiss my husband's lips or any part of his body again," Clarissa hissed at Lenora through gritted teeth. She then whipped her head around at Dalziel. "Wipe your mouth," she commanded.

He did.

Lenora had an incredulous expression on her face. "Well, I see you have taken up with a hedge-born slu—"

"Bite your tongue or I will cut it out." Dalziel's eyes burned with anger. Lenora bit back her derogatory remark, gave him an evil stare, then stormed off.

"Honestly, Dalziel, sometimes you can be such a wild Scotsman." His mother meant it as an insult.

"That's because I am one. Now, if you will excuse us. My wife and I have much to do." He ushered Clarissa ahead of him and walked past his mother.

They were halfway across the hall when Clarissa muttered under her breath, "Well, they seem like charming people."

Dalziel burst out laughing.

THE EVENING WAS WINDING down, and Dalziel and Clarissa prepared to take their leave. It had been a taxing evening, trying to keep out of the same circles as Lenora and his mother. Now he just wanted to spend time alone, at home, in bed, with his wife, and preferably inside her.

They were moving towards the door when Davenport approached.

"I did not know you are Minerva's boy," he said, referring to Dalziel's mother.

"I'm not. I am Jacob Robertson's son. He raised me alone. My mother had no hand in it."

"All right steady on, I did not mean any harm." Davenport replied then leered at Clarissa. "I do not believe we have been formally introduced, my dear."

"You haven't." Dalziel clasped Clarissa's hand and pulled her out the door. There was no way he wanted Davenport to get his dirty, debauched paws on his wife.

"That was rather rude, Dalziel. Whatever will he think now," Clarissa said.

"I dinnae care, Sweeting."

Dependents

DALZIEL WAS WORKING in his study and still reeling from his mother and Lenora's appearance at the assembly the previous night. He knew if they were in town; they were both up to no good. He did not know how Lenora had recruited his mother's support.

It was no surprise when Mr. Bell announced his mother was waiting to see him. He knew it was most likely to do with her annuity, and Dalziel preferred a witness when he dealt with his mother. He asked Mr. Bell to fetch Rupert. When Rupert arrived, he made him sit at the desk, then Mr. Bell directed his mother into the study.

"What do you want, *màthair*?"

"I ask about my annuity, which was put aside by my dearest papa."

"What about it?"

"Son, is it really necessary for us to speak with a servant present?" She referred to Rupert.

"He is my clerk, and aye it tis, he does the accounts, so he needs to be here. The other alternative is my wife, Lady Stanhope, she can also assist you if you prefer. Take your pick."

"Lady, is she? I highly doubt it after the wine throwing incident. It mortified poor Lenora."

"Lenora will get over it. Now, what do you want?" Dalziel asked.

"I'd like an increase in my allowance," Minerva replied.

"What for, and how much?"

"It is unseemly to discuss my financial needs in front of others." She eyed Rupert again.

"Ma, you have two choices. Make your petition with Rupert in the room or leave."

"Very well. I need twice the amount. I have a lifestyle to maintain and a social standing, which means I have social events to attend and they are very expensive."

Dalziel said, "No. Downsize and socialize less."

"But I am already practically a pauper."

"Paupers cannot afford servants and social events."

"I see you've turned out just like your father," she bit out.

"Aye, and proud I am of it," Dalziel replied.

Rupert cleared his throat. "My lord, do you really need me here for this?"

"Aye," Dalziel replied.

"No," his mother said at the same time.

She stood and paced the room. "You still cannot forgive me for leaving your father, can you? It was years ago. What did you expect me to do, live in the stinking Highlands forever?"

"Aye, those were the vows you took." Dalziel banged his fist on the desk.

"You do not understand. I deserved so much more than a stronghold in the middle of nowhere. I was made to be courted by kings, not surrounded by common folk with strange habits. And the Scots treated me like a pariah. They will no doubt do the same to your wife too." His mother pouted.

"So why aren't you courting kings now? Where is your rich Anglian nobleman?" Dalziel asked.

His mother glowered at him. "Never mind. I see you will never understand."

"Aye, *Màthair*, I will never understand how you abandoned a three-year-old boy."

He saw a flash of regret in her eyes before she masked it with indifference.

"I see this will do me no good. You have grown into a tyrant, and I am leaving." On those words, she quit the room.

Dalziel watched her go whilst Rupert noisily gathered his things to leave. "Well, thank you for interrupting my hot lunch, which has now gone cold just so I could witness a family squabble I did not need to be present for," Rupert grumbled.

Dalziel just said, "Get out."

Harmony

CLARISSA WAS DOING paperwork in her solar when she had an unexpected visitor. Harmony Durham called. Clarissa was happy to see her, and after a brief exchange, they sat down to enjoy refreshments.

"How have you been Harmony?"

"Oh, I have been very well. Just keeping myself busy with Lily."

"And how is Lily doing? Is she still latching on to people's ankles?" Clarissa asked.

Harmony smiled but did not answer.

"Harmony, have you not heard any word from Cedric at all?"

"No, none. And the shire-reeve has not been around to ask either."

"Hmm, I just hope he is safe wherever he is," Clarissa replied.

Harmony scanned the solar and the view of the sizeable gardens outside.

"You must be happy to have married so well. I mean, you will not have to work so hard now that you have a rich man for a husband," Harmony said while nibbling on a slice of cake.

"I agree life has become somewhat better."

"And how is the *Cause,* Clarissa? Are you managing without Cedric?"

"Yes, all is well. But it would be better if Cedric were here."

"And have you any other rescue plans? Will you be down at the docks again soon?" Harmony asked.

Clarissa just stared at Harmony for some time, feigning a smile. Harmony had never cared much for the details before. Clarissa just nodded and assured her it was all arranged.

When Harmony took her leave, Clarissa was relieved. She could not put her finger on it, but something had changed between them.

Grand Master

WHEN DALZIEL FINISHED seeing to land matters, he went in search of his wife. He found her with her hair unbound and barefoot in the garden. She wore a long kirtle, and she was deep in thought.

Dalziel walked over to her, hauled her over his shoulder, and marched straight to their chambers. Clarissa squealed, then started giggling.

"What are we doing here?" she asked when he placed her on her feet in his room.

"I ache, Wife, and I need release and you're going to give it to me."

"But tis daytime." Her eyes rounded in shock.

"Aye, what of it?"

"The sun is out." She pointed at the window.

"And?"

"People only couple at night," she replied.

Dalziel realized she was being serious, and he burst out laughing.

Clarissa whacked his arm. "Do not laugh at me." She frowned.

"I'm sorry, my love, but tis no specific time to engage in coupling, especially when we are married." His eyes danced with humor.

"Really?" she asked in amazement.

"Tis sorry I am that I had not taught you this lesson earlier. I will have to train you several times a day, so you ken your lesson well."

"Oh, you think you are a master at this, do you?"

"I am a Grand Master." He winked.

She placed her hands on her hips. "You should not boast about such things, Lord Stanhope!"

"Quiet, Lady Stanhope, I have much mastering to do to you."

Several hours later Clarissa had been well and truly mastered on every available surface in the room.

Chapter 8 – The Past

Lenora

Clarissa was out at the *cove* all morning, helping some women settle in. She had also arranged better locks for the doors and ways of keeping the occupants safe at night.

It was midday when she returned home, and she felt a weird tension.

Mrs. Armstrong came running to her straight away when she entered the main door.

"Mistress, there's an obnoxious Lenora woman in your solar. I would serve her tea, but I'd likely spit in it. She wants to see the master and said she willna leave until he arrives."

"Tis all right, I will deal with it. Thank you."

Clarissa noticed the servants hovering outside the doorway pretending to dust. She just rolled her eyes.

One thing that struck Clarissa when she walked into the solar was how stunning Lenora was. She had a sultry air about her and confidence to match. They were the traits needed to survive in a harsh world as a paramour, and as much as she detested the woman, she had to admit she could see the appeal to a man like Dalziel.

But Dalziel was hers now, and it was time Lenora was apprised of that fact.

She observed Lenora poke around her things as if she were searching for something.

"Can I help you with anything?" Clarissa gave her a winning smile.

Lenora jumped in fright, then hesitated. She had not expected a friendly welcome. It was as if she retracted her claws for a split second, unsure how to proceed.

Clarissa had learned in her long life, there was more than one way to disarm an enemy.

Lenora rallied and replied, "Aye, there is something you can do. Please tell Dalziel *his lover* is here. I believe he is expecting me."

Clarissa heard someone gasp in outrage from the doorway, and she glared at them to get back to work. The maid immediately returned to dusting the same spot she had been dusting for the last five minutes.

"My husband is not in right now. If you tell me what matters you wish to discuss, mayhap I can pass the message along... later tonight, after he and I have finished making love... for several hours." She gave Lenora a smug smile.

Clarissa saw a flash of irritation in Lenora's eyes before she said, "I prefer to wait."

"I'm afraid tis not possible. I have callers coming in today, and I need the room cleared for their arrival."

Lenora took a turn about the room in a leisurely manner, and Clarissa knew she was sharpening her claws. "I suppose you think you are clever, Lady Stanhope. Let me tell you, Dalziel always comes back to me. The only reason he married you is because of the work he does for the king of Scotland. When he is done here, you'll be nothing but a used-up English whore." She smirked.

What work does Dalziel do for the Scottish king? Clarissa wondered but filed it away for a later time. She replied, "Well then, I best make the most of my whoring skills while he's still in my bed because he really enjoys it."

Clarissa knew that remark scored a hit because Lenora's face twisted in rage. Lenora changed tack. She walked up to Clarissa and asked, "So tell me, how does he do it with you? Does he tie you down with ropes or just the spankings? You ken he loves to inflict pain."

Clarissa flinched and seemed uncertain. Lenora took that as her cue to aim for the jugular.

She chuckled. "Oh, my dear, what an innocent you are. Do you mean Dalziel has never played with you yet? He has never tied you down to the bed and brought you to the brink of pain to give you pleasure?"

Clarissa faltered. She realized she still knew nothing about her husband or his sexual proclivities.

Lenora knew she had hit her mark. She now stood in front of Clarissa and said, "Oh, tis true then. He has hidden his most base nature from you." She caressed Clarissa's cheek, then whispered, "You will never satisfy him."

Clarissa slapped Lenora's hand away.

"Leave now, before I throw you out," Mr. Bell boomed from the doorway. His eyes like daggers.

"Oh, I am leaving, and you'll be sorry you ever crossed me, Clarissa," Lenora hissed before she sashayed past with her nose stuck high in the air.

Finch's Tavern, Bamburgh

AFTER LENORA LEFT, Clarissa felt out of sorts. The barbs had struck true, and doubt festered, breaking down her fragile ego. She wondered if Dalziel was holding back parts of himself from her. Clarissa headed to the one place she felt safe. Finch's Tavern. There, she could drown her sorrows and forget about being his wife for a few hours.

Several hours later, Clarissa was well and truly drunk. But she had won a little money. Something she never played for, except today. When she thought about Lenora, she cringed at the pain of knowing Dalziel would probably leave her and she would need funds to live on.

She was depressed just thinking about being alone, heartbroken, and mired in debt while Lenora cavorted with her husband.

"Come on, Love. Time to go home," Dalziel said.

"Dee... elsh?" she slurred and squinted with one eye open at the blurred vision of a man who sounded like her husband.

"Aye, tis me, Love."

"How did shoo findsh me?"

Dalziel bent down and picked her up off the chair, settling her in his arms.

"Marley Finch sent a message to Toby, who sent a message to Jean-Luc, who sent a message to Mrs. Armstrong who told me to come and fetch ye."

"Thash nishe of Marley."

"Aye, tis very nice of Mrs. Finch, especially since you've occupied her good table pouring your heart out about a Scotsman and stealer of women's hearts." He grinned.

Clarissa reached into her pocket and pulled out several *sceats*. "I won shom shilver sho I can leaves shoo," she slurred before she passed out.

Dalziel chuckled and carried her out the door. *Daft woman*. He kissed her hair, then said, "You are not leaving me that easily, Wife."

He carried her out the back door of the tavern while Marley Finch fussed over her. He paid Marley the coin for her troubles and then took his precious bundle home.

Last Rites

THE FOLLOWING MORNING, Clarissa awoke with a pounding in her head and ringing in her ears. The room was spinning. Her mouth tasted like ash and she smelled like a brewery. She opened her eyes and moaned in pain from the piercing bright lights, then shut them again.

Clutching her stomach, she felt the bile building and nausea set in. She swallowed to keep it down.

"Somebody, help me, I'm dying," she groaned. "Call the bishop. I need last rites... last rites!"

Dalziel chuckled. "You're not dying, Ris. You've just had a wee bit too much ale. Now here, sit up and drink this." He pulled her up, so she was sitting against the headboard, then pushed something towards her lips.

Water, it was fresh water, and it tasted heavenly to her parched throat. Clarissa drank two cups.

"I'll keep the curtains drawn and there's a pot beside the bed if you need it. Come down for tea and dry toast when you're ready. We have a lot to discuss."

"Aye, thank you, Husband," Clarissa replied before she burst into tears.

"Och Ris, dinnae cry." Dalziel tugged her into his arms and lay down on the bed with her.

Clarissa burrowed her face into his neck. "I will never drink again for as long as I live because if this is not hell, I do not know what is."

Dalziel kissed her forehead and chuckled. "You'll live, Sweeting."

Submission

THAT NIGHT WHEN SHE was freshly bathed, fed, and hydrated, Clarissa was tucked up against Dalziel and the insecurities came to her again.

"When you are with me, do you wish I was someone else?" she asked.

"No, never. Mr. Bell told me about Lenora's visit and believe me, she will never set foot in our home again."

"Lenora told me you prefer a different type of loving, with ropes and pain." She blushed.

He stiffened and cursed, "I am going to kill that fucking woman!"

"Tis true then. I will never fully satisfy you." She gave him big doe eyes.

"Are you jesting? I *love* you, you annoying woman, and every time we couple tis the best it has ever been for me."

Clarissa took a sharp intake of breath and whispered, "You love me?"

"Of course, I do." Dalziel was agitated and sat up, dragging her with him. "What the bloody hell do you think I am doing here?"

Clarissa had an enormous grin on her face. "Really? But what of the ropes and the pain? Do you seek others for that?" Her smile vanished.

"No, I dinnae seek anyone else. You satisfy me, Wife."

"Are there things you've done with other women that you won't do with me?" Clarissa knew she sounded unreasonable, but she could not let it go.

Dalziel sounded exasperated. "You ken I was not a virgin when I married you, and I dinnae want to discuss any other woman in our bed."

Clarissa turned away and tried to hide her disappointment.

Dalziel sighed, then turned her to face him. They passed a few moments in silence before he said, "In my line of work, I face many dangers, and often I needed a release from the worry and pressure that builds."

Clarissa nodded her head while absent-mindedly caressing his chest. Dalziel loved that about her. She was not aware she did it often.

"Sometimes in the past, the best way for me to relieve that pressure was to dominate a woman while we coupled."

Clarissa's eyes widened in shock as she asked, "Did you hurt them?"

"No, *never*. Tis not like that."

"Then explain it to me, please. I will not judge."

"Sometimes I take pleasure in having a woman naked and tied to the bed so she cannot move. She is blindfolded so she cannot see. All she can do is submit to me and feel whatever I do to her."

"And these women... they enjoyed that?" Clarissa sounded uncertain.

"Aye, or I would never have done it."

Clarissa was quiet for some time, and Dalziel worried. He had never opened up to someone he loved regarding this side of his preferences.

"Then why have you never done those things with me?" she whined.

"I honestly have not felt the need."

"Oh." She sounded forlorn.

"What the hell are you sad about now, Love?" Dalziel was growing frustrated. This was unfamiliar territory for him. Talking to a woman was exhausting.

"Because I feel you are not giving me all of you. Others have shared that part of you but me." She pouted.

Dalziel was done with the conversation. If his wife needed proof of how well she satisfied him, then he would give her what she needed.

"Love, you have *all* of me. Every inch and every part of my heart. That is something no other woman has ever received from me. But if you want me to show you, then I will happily oblige."

Her emerald eyes turned seductive as she licked her lips, and Dalziel was undone.

He got out of bed. "I am going to get some ties. When I return, I want you naked on your back in bed. Your legs spread wide and your arms holding the headboard. Do it now," he commanded.

Dalziel left the room and when he returned with leather ties, his wife was spread out before him like a magnificent offering. The thought that she obeyed him immediately made him hard.

"Do you trust me?" he asked.

"Yes."

"If you feel discomfort at all, say 'Stop' and I will."

She nodded her head in eagerness.

Dalziel tied her wrists to the head of the bed and her ankles to the lower rungs. She was completely exposed to his gaze and at his mercy.

Then he placed a blindfold over her eyes.

Dalziel stood over her, naked and aroused. This was like nothing he had ever experienced before. It was visceral and powerful because the woman being dominated was the love of his life and he would make it special for her.

"Close your eyes and just feel what I do to you."

Dalziel spent the next hour ravishing every inch of her with his mouth and hands until she was moaning in ecstasy. Clarissa tried to pull free of the binds but could not. Her eyes covered, all she could do was feel and submit. The anticipation of the unknown heightened her senses, and she felt on edge, breathless and wanton.

Then Clarissa felt Dalziel's body brace above her before he gave her his weight. He cradled his hips within her sweet spot and nestled against her core.

Dalziel was burning with lust; he was painfully aroused. He felt like a conqueror as he dominated his captive to his will. He held all the control, but really it was Clarissa who held all the power. Unable to wait any longer, Dalziel thrust between her thighs and pounded inside her heated core. She was like a treasure offered for his pleasure and privilege, at his mercy, and her trust humbled him.

He drove deep, claiming and conquering. Hearing her moans and screams of pleasure as she shuddered beneath him. When he had brought her to completion several times, only then did he seek his release as he came with a groan. It had been the most satisfying experience, bar none.

During the night, after several bouts of lovemaking. They were talking in hushed whispers, when Clarissa asked, "Why did you end your arrangement with Lenora?"

"Love, I dinnae want to talk about her in our bed."

"Please, I promise I'll never ask again, but I'm just curious."

"At first it was fun and exciting, trying new things with an experienced woman. She enjoyed being submissive to my dominant nature. She always needed pain for her pleasure."

"What kind of pain?"

She preferred a hard spanking, but later she requested cutting into the skin to achieve her peak. I was not prepared to go that far. It was abhorrent to me." Dalziel paused and recalled something about her.

"What is it?" Clarissa asked.

"She used to have these pins she would heat to pierce the skin. I refused to partake of anything like that and I kenned that was the beginning of the end. She found others to satisfy her dark cravings because by then I could not stomach being around her." He sighed. "Why do you keep insisting we talk of her?"

"I wanted to make sure whatever was between you both was over," Clarissa replied.

"Trust me, Love, we were well and truly finished by then and when I saw you in that Town Hall, no other woman existed for me."

Clarissa grinned and planted a kiss on his lips. "Good answer, Husband."

Chapter 9 - The Letters

A Son

It had been three weeks since Clarissa and Dalziel had consummated their marriage.

Clarissa was passing time before she was to attend a lady's soiree with some women of the shire. She hated such events, but they were necessary for keeping up appearances and keeping within the good graces of the locals. She was trying to embroider some handkerchiefs, but if her battered, bloodied thumb was any indication of success, she was failing.

Martin appeared at the door in the solar. "Beg your pardon, Mistress, tis urgent."

Clarissa immediately stood. "What is it?"

"Tis Elsa. We need you at the *cove*."

Clarissa paled. "I'll come at once."

Because of the recent rain, the road was treacherous to travel and took longer than expected. When she rounded the *cove*, she dismounted and tethered her horse. Clarissa ran into the large double-story abode. It was built into the cliff side and surrounded by trees, hidden from view. It was also their *safe house*. The place she and Cedric had built together out of necessity. When she arrived, they were waiting for her.

"My lady, follow me." It was Martha, Elsa's maid.

Clarissa approached Elsa's room. When she stepped inside, she wanted to weep. Elsa lay on the bed, beaten and bruised and wheezing through broken ribs.

"What the hell happened?" Clarissa cried.

"Davenport. Elsa went to her house to retrieve parchments from the office, and he was home. Twas lucky Jean-Luc went to check on her or she would be dead," Martin said.

"Clar...Clarissa, is that you?" Elsa asked through a split lip.

"Aye, I'm here."

"I am sorry. I did not mean to bring trouble. I need my letters from my house."

"Was it worth risking your life?" Clarissa asked.

"Aye, I have a son. Davenport has kept him from me for the past two years. The letters will help me get him back," Elsa replied then began to cry.

"Shh, do not worry, I will see to it." Clarissa sat by her bedside and promised she would find Elsa's son.

10pm, Davenport's Study, Bamburgh

CLARISSA FUMBLED AROUND the study. She had planned her break-in meticulously. There was a rowdy house party in progress with scantily clad participants milling about. She had worn a revealing dress with a hood, then snuck away when no one was scrutinizing her movements. The plan was simple: straight in and straight out.

Clarissa recalled Elsa's instructions. *"Behind the desk third row of books, family bible."* She found it. She lifted it off the shelf and opened it up. It was hollowed out and in the middle were parchments folded inside. The other instructions for the letters were, *"Key hanging under the desk, unlock the second drawer, lift the false bottom."*

She fumbled around under the desk, felt the key hanging on a hook, opened the drawer, and fished out the letters, then returned the key to its hiding place.

Clarissa had just stuffed everything into her dress when she heard footsteps down the hall.

She turned to flee and crashed head-first into an irate Dalziel.

"What the fuck are you doing here?" he hissed. "Do you have any idea the danger you are in? Davenport is on his way."

Dalziel grabbed her arm and pulled her towards him. "Play along," he demanded as he spun her around, so her back was against the wall, and he covered her with his body. She stared into his blazing eyes. His jaw was clenched when his lips connected with hers. She stiffened.

"Relax, sweeting, follow my lead," Dalziel nipped at her lips. "Open for me," he said.

She did. His tongue sought entrance. Clarissa became lost in the embrace and closed her eyes. Gentle yet demanding, Dalziel stoked her passion into a roaring inferno. He bit her lip, and she whimpered.

Dalziel closed his eyes and drowned in the sensation of his wife. He felt all of her abundant curves in his arms. *And what the hell was she wearing?* He deepened the kiss, struggling to hold it together. He aligned his body to hers as she moved closer to him.

She was breathless from the kiss. "What are ye doing?"

"We need to appear as if we are coupling," he replied.

With that, Dalziel loosened his trews, partially exposing his backside. He lifted her off the ground, so she straddled his waist, her thighs exposed on both sides. Her skirt up in the air.

"Moan, sweetheart," he demanded.

He began pumping his hips against her covered center and groaning. He was hard as a rock, and she was thoroughly aroused each time his hardened length hit her pleasure spot. Although it was supposed to be a ruse, they were not acting. The passion between them was real. His breathing became shallow, and he grunted.

Dalziel wished he could take his wife against the wall for real, but they were in danger.

He had come to the house party intending to search Davenport's study and was surprised to find his wife there.

A door opened behind them, and the voices of several men drifted inside. They stopped talking, then he heard a voice say, "Dalziel? You old fox, are you swiving someone back there?"

"Whatever will your wife think?" Lancet asked.

Clarissa was aware of other men entering the room. She hid her face in Dalziel's neck.

He held her tight, grunted a few times while she made a loud moaning sound, and then he lowered her to the ground as he pulled up his trews. He covered her from view.

Dalziel spoke over his shoulder to the men in the room. "I apologize. I assumed this room was empty. Some privacy, if you will. I dinnae want to embarrass the lady."

"Is that Lady Lewis back there with you? Have you been jabbing your sword in her scabbard?" Davenport heckled, and the men chuckled at his ribald joke.

Clarissa stiffened and raised an eyebrow at the mention of a Lady Lewis. Dalziel raised an eyebrow in return.

"Go now," he whispered to Clarissa. "Put on your hood and keep your head down. Head to my carriage outside and wait for me." He then turned to face the men and ushered her out of the doorway.

Chamberlain reached out and whacked Clarissa's bottom as she passed by, and Dalziel almost killed him on the spot. Clarissa bolted out the door and ran to the entranceway.

"Gentlemen. I am sorry, but a man has urges he must satisfy." Dalziel leisurely refastened his trews and headed towards the decanter to pour himself a drink. He scanned the desk to make sure there was nothing out of place.

"What a pity you did not ask the lady to join us. I'm sure we could have all accommodated her, or we would not have minded watching," Lancet said, with a salacious glint in his eye.

Dalziel's lips twitched. "I dinnae share *my* woman."

Davenport scoffed, "All women are made for sharing."

Dalziel laughed, but inside he wanted to punch the man in the throat. These were unscrupulous men, and he was thankful his wife was not caught in here alone with any of them.

TWENTY MINUTES LATER, Dalziel joined Clarissa inside his conveyance. He stepped in and slammed the door, then hit the roof twice to signal they leave. As they moved, he glared at Clarissa. "What the devil did you think you were doing in there?"

She opened her mouth to answer then closed it again.

"Do you ken how dangerous that was?"

She looked contrite.

"You told me you were off to a harmless soiree with the ladies. My arse!" he shouted. "What were you doing there?" He sat across from her, but he was livid.

"I was trying to …" She fumbled to search for an answer and bit her lip.

What Clarissa did not realize is Dalziel knew when she was lying, she had a tell. She always bit her bottom lip and chewed.

"Dinnae lie to me!" he yelled. Dalziel was losing it. To think his wife had placed herself in danger, she was reckless, oblivious to the dangers in that house and tonight of all nights when he was closing in on his target. This was not what he signed up for. He was supposed to get a biddable, boring wife, and he got anything but.

"You will tell me what you were doing in there, Wife, and what parchments you have hidden in your garment."

"I was searching for a bible passage—"

"Ris," Dalziel growled in a low voice.

Clarissa sighed. "Tis just letters."

"Show me."

"No."

"So, help me, Wife, if you dinnae show me now, I will strip you naked and search you myself. The choice is yours."

Clarissa blushed. "You would not dare?"

"I have licked every inch of your body. Do you think I would not strip you naked right here?"

They sat in complete silence, neither moving, and then Dalziel lunged at her.

"All right, I'll show you!" she yelled. Both hands were up in front of her to stop him from coming closer.

Dalziel relaxed back into his seat and lifted his hand, palm open, towards her.

Clarissa huffed. "Honestly, you are the most infuriating, cumbersome, high handed..." She ranted incoherently and reluctantly pulled out the parchments from her dress and handed it over. She folded her arms and glared at her husband.

Under any other circumstance, Dalziel would have laughed. She was adorable when she was riled. But right now, was no laughing matter.

He opened the parchment and read. It was Davenport's Will and there was a codicil about a boy, something to do with property and inheritance. Dalziel knew there was so much more to this tale.

"Who is the boy in this Will?" he asked.

"No one," she replied, biting her lip.

Damn it. Dalziel swore to himself. She was keeping secrets.

"Hand over the letters."

She huffed and retrieved a bundle of letters.

He flicked through them, but nothing struck him as odd, although it was mostly in French and again some mention of a child named 'Jordan.'

"What do you ken about these?"

"Nothing. I have never seen them before. I was merely retrieving them for a friend," Clarissa replied.

"Who's your friend?" Dalziel asked.

"Tis none of your concern. I promised I would not tell."

"But I am your husband."

Clarissa snorted.

They remained in a silent stare-off. Neither one spoke nor said anything.

"Tell me why you have stolen Davenport's Will, Clarissa."

She shook her head.

Dalziel's eyes blazed with rage. "Ris, this is not a game. Davenport is a dangerous man."

Clarissa crossed her arms over her chest and pursed her lips tighter. Then a thought came to her. "Why were *you* there, Husband? Were you searching for something too or were you meeting up with *someone*... say a Lady Lewis?"

Dalziel gritted his teeth. How much did he divulge to his wife, and how much did he trust her? The Will and the letters made him suspicious. *What if she had something to do with Siward?*

He needed to compromise, swap information.

"I work for King Macbeth of Scotland and my task is to ken what goes on behind closed doors."

"And that takes you to parties with scantily clad women?" She raised her brow in disbelief.

"Aye."

"Now who's lying?" Clarissa replied and stared out the window. She was having suspicions about her husband and his fidelity.

"Clarissa, you court danger with your nightly activities, and I will not let it continue. You either tell me the truth so I can help, or you will face the consequences."

Clarissa tried not to flinch at his words. She still had to decide whether she trusted her husband enough to tell him everything. The mere fact he was at a party cavorting with the same men who beat their wives did not bode well for the *Cause*. So, she kept her lips sealed.

That night, she slept alone in her chambers.

Dalziel also preferred it that way. Clarissa's refusal to give him any information meant he needed to tread carefully. He needed distance so he could think straight, and for the first time since their marriage was consummated, he locked his bedroom door.

<hr />

CLARISSA DELIVERED Elsa's parchments to the *cove*. She had not spoken to her husband since the carriage ride two nights ago, and she preferred it that way. She had made some inquiries about where Dalziel went at night and, after learning of 'The Three Lords', she asked Jean-Luc about the establishment. He told her it was a part brothel, part gaming den for the wealthy men.

Clarissa's heart burned with jealously and then with sadness. She decided she no longer wanted any part of his genuine marriage and planned on living her own life separately. Which is what she should have done in the beginning before succumbing to lust. She had learned in her line of work that men could speak words of love to their wives while keeping lovers on the side. At least she never told him she loved him in return. *A stupid man was not worth the sentiment.*

Elsa Davenport was so grateful to have the Will and the letters. She thanked Clarissa over and over. She planned on retrieving her son, Jordan, who she nicknamed Jordie, and moving to France. Jean-Luc and Pierre were more than happy to help her.

Sometime later Clarissa was sitting in her office at the *safe house*, going over the bag of correspondence Martin had dropped off that morning when something struck her as odd. There was a blank note for Cedric in the bag with an address in *Glencoe* Scotland, but no name.

The strange thing was Clarissa had seen that same address on a parchment sitting in Davenport's desk drawer. It was in a bundle with other letters but not part of the parchments Elsa requested. Maybe if she got hold of that bundle, she would find out more.

Returning to the Scene of the Crime

CLARISSA ENTERED THE side of the large mansion. The door was unlocked, thanks to a servant. She wielded her dirk.

"This is dangerous, Cousin. If you get caught, you could end up in the dungeons," Pierre said.

Clarissa ignored him. "Just keep a lookout. *Il ne faut rien laisser au hazard."–Leave nothing to chance.*

"Bien sûr."—Of course. Pierre grumbled and took up his position as the lookout.

Clarissa made her way into Davenport's study. Retrieved the key and opened the second draw. The letter was on top and not inside the false bottom. It was perfumed and mentioned something about a White Bear. She wondered what this had to do with Cedric.

She grabbed the compact bundle tied with ribbon and stuffed it into the pocket of her trews. She was just heading out the doorway when she was startled by Davenport himself. He was drunk and stumbled into the study, then collapsed onto the settee. Davenport had not seen her. He lay down with his eyes closed.

Clarissa quietly walked over to his side and just studied him. *What kind of animal beat a woman?*

He opened his eyes in surprise. "Who the devil are you?" he asked.

When Clarissa peered down at him, all she saw were the bruises and broken bones of countless women like Elsa and Sally and her mother. Then she saw her father's smug, entitled face.

Before Davenport could move, Clarissa lifted her dirk and stabbed him in the thigh. Then she hissed, "That is for all the women you hurt, you useless prick."

He was writhing in pain with blood pouring from the wound.

Clarissa stabbed him again, this time in the upper arm. He rolled onto the settee, trying to get away from her. As with all abusing cowards, he would not fight back when faced with a stronger opponent.

Clarissa threw a cloth at him and said, "Staunch the bleeding and stop crying you sack of pig shit!"

Then she turned and ran.

Where Were You?

CLARISSA STUMBLED INTO her chamber after midnight and lit a candle. She went behind the partition, stripped naked, and washed using the water and basin. Clarissa dried herself and walked towards her bed. She had just slipped on her chemise when she jumped at the sound of an angry voice.

"Where were you?"

Dalziel was sitting in the darkened corner of her room. *How long had he been there?*

"I was out."

"Out where, Clarissa?" his voice was menacing.

"Um..."

Dalziel was out of the chair and across the room in a heartbeat. She shuffled backward until her back came up against the wall.

Dalziel placed one hand on either side of her shoulders, effectively caging her against the wall. "Did I not tell you to stay away from other men?"

"I was not with other men." She bit her lip and chewed.

There was silence between them.

"Right, I guess I am going to have to remind you of who you be*long to*."

Dalziel's lips came crashing down on hers. He devoured her mouth with his lips and tongue, then pulled away to say, "These lips are mine and belong to no other."

He tore her chemise off, and his mouth latched onto a breast as he suckled. Then he released it with a popping sound. He lavished all his attention on its twin. His hands caressing her while he laved the tips with his tongue. "These are mine and belong to no other," he growled.

Clarissa was drowning in a sea of sensual pleasure, heightened by the dominant power her husband unleashed. She had no choice but to submit to his control.

One hand clasped her center as he rubbed her core until she was glistening. "This is mine and belongs to no other," Dalziel snarled.

Clarissa was breathless. Her mind was losing traction.

"I swear, Husband, I have not been with anyone else," she said between moans. Drowning in a veritable onslaught of sensations.

"Make sure it stays that way."

Clarissa gazed at her husband. He reminded her of a feral creature. An alpha staking his claim on a mate. He pulled her away from the wall and pushed her forward until she was bent over the bed. Her hands gripped the linens while her feet remained on the floor. Her naked backside was exposed to his view.

Dalziel brought his hand down hard and slapped her bottom. It was firm, but not painful. "That's for putting yourself in danger," he seethed.

He spanked her again. "That's for making me worry."

Clarissa's eyes glazed over with arousal when she felt his hands massaging her intimately. He was dominating her, but she did not fear him.

Dalziel stood behind her and nudged her feet further apart. He unfastened his trews and released his hardened length as one hand gently massaged her core.

Clarissa felt pins and needles prickling up her spine. She pushed back against him.

Dalziel's voice sounded gravelly when he said, "I need to claim what's mine; it has been too long."

"Do it," she replied in a sultry voice.

Dalziel gripped her hips, positioned and slammed into her from behind. Clarissa moaned at the invasion. He was so large it set off a flutter of contractions.

Dalziel gave her a moment to adjust. Then he pounded into her. The sound of bare flesh slapping against flesh, and loud moans were heard throughout the entire chamber, and neither participant cared.

They were lost in a haze of pent-up release. The tension had been building between them for days. Dalziel pulled her into a standing position, till she was on tiptoes as he continued to angle and thrust into her for behind. One hand pinched a nipple while the other stroked her center. Clarissa rested the back of her head on his shoulder. He bit her neck and nipped at her earlobe, whispering sweet nothings in her ear.

It was a sensory overload. She reached behind her and gripped the back of his head so she could move his lips closer to hers. She climaxed just as Dalziel swallowed her scream with a searing kiss before he exploded inside her.

They collapsed onto the bed, gasping for air. Dalziel pulled her against him and held her tight.

"You are mine, Ris and I will kill any man who thinks to touch you."

Clarissa shuddered at the deadly intent in his eyes.

"Tis only you, Husband, I promise."

"Good."

She waited a while, then nudged him in the rib with her elbow. "And what of you?"

"Tis only you, Wife, I promise."

"Then why were you at The Three Lords?" she asked.

Dalziel stilled. "Tis not for the reasons you think."

Clarissa saw the truth in his eyes and was satisfied with that answer. "Make sure it stays that way or I will kill any woman who thinks to touch what is *mine*." She scowled.

Dalziel burst out laughing and gathered her against his chest.

Blunt force

THE FOLLOWING MORNING, Clarissa sat at the breakfast table sipping her tea, wondering why Dalziel kept staring at her. "What?" she asked.

"Davenport was murdered last night. The news is all over town."

Clarissa froze momentarily, about to take another sip. She met Dalziel's eyes and knew he was asking her a question.

"Oh, really? That's terrible," she replied, trying to remain calm.

"Aye, they found him in a pool of blood."

Clarissa panicked. That could not be. The thigh wound was not as deep neither was his arm wound.

"Blood? How mortifying was he attacked?" she asked nonchalantly.

"Blunt force to the head. It caved his skull in," Dalziel replied.

Clarissa relaxed knowing whoever killed Davenport did it after she left.

"You dinnae appear surprised, love, is there a reason why?" Dalziel asked.

"The man had a lot of enemies." She shrugged.

Dalziel finished his toast and wiped his mouth. "I heard someone saw your horse near his house last night."

She stilled midway to biting into her toast.

Dalziel's eyes were blazing. "What did I tell you about going there, Ris?"

"I swear to you, Husband, he was alive when I left."

"Why the hell did you go back there, tis dangerous?" Dalziel slammed his fist on the table.

"Husband, twas not me, I swear it!" Clarissa implored.

"What was the state in which you left him then?"

"He was alive, and his skull was in perfect condition."

Chapter 10 – Half-Truths

Missing Things

It was a couple of days since Davenport's murder. Clarissa was searching the house and gardens for her mother's gold chain. She asked Mrs. Armstrong and the servants, who said they had seen no chain. She knew it must just be somewhere in the house and would turn up, eventually. Thinking nothing more of it, Clarissa went about her day.

Later that morning, she noticed her wax seal from her solar was also missing. Mrs. Armstrong helped her search as well, but to no avail. Clarissa assumed they were most likely in her office at the *safe house*, and she intended to search there later in the week. She then went about her day, focusing on the myriad of tasks she had to complete.

Little did Clarissa know these missing things would be the catalyst for an oncoming storm, and the damage it would leave in its wake would be catastrophic.

Shire-Reeve

IT WAS 2PM THAT SAME afternoon when Mr. Bell came to find Clarissa.

"Lady Clarissa, the Bamburgh shire-reeve, Mr. Bernard Smith is here to speak to you."

"What about?"

"I do not know, but I think it would be best if you waited for the master to get home before speaking to these men," Mr. Bell replied.

"Men? Who is with him?" Clarissa asked.

"An Edmund Snape."

She shuddered. "I despise the man, but I am curious why they are both here. Let them in. I'll meet them in the drawing room."

"I strongly advise against it, my lady." Mr. Bell urged her to reconsider.

"What if you remain in the doorway, Mr. Bell, so if there's any trouble, you can assist me?"

He thought on it for a while, then sighed and agreed.

Dalziel was out on estate matters and so Clarissa prepared the best she could and received them in her drawing room.

What she was not prepared for was the hostility she encountered from Edmund Snape.

"Pardon the intrusion, Lady Stanhope, but we have come on urgent matters regarding the death of a gentleman," Bernard Smith said.

Clarissa refused to flinch. She remained calm and greeted them both, then politely asked them to sit.

"I cannot imagine what this has to do with me?" she replied.

"Liar," Snape muttered under his breath.

"I beg your pardon, but why is Mr. Snape here?" she asked Bernard.

"As the *tithing-man* and respected member of society, he is here with allegations against you."

"What type of allegations?"

"Murder," Snape hissed.

Clarissa stiffened. "What are you suggesting?" She glared at Bernard, ignoring Snape.

"You..." Bernard cleared his throat. "You were seen near the vicinity of Lord Davenport's house on the night he was killed."

"But that is ridiculous."

"I saw you there," Snape said.

"Oh, please enlighten me, Mr. Snape, because I do not have any notion what you are talking about." Clarissa folded her arms and waited.

"Very well, Clarissa," Snape began.

"Tis, Lady Stanhope to you!" Mr. Bell yelled from the doorway. Clarissa noticed he held a sword loosely in one hand. *Where on earth did Mr. Bell get a sword?*

Snape paled slightly and amended, "Very well, Lady Stanhope, I saw your horse nearby."

Clarissa burst out laughing. "A horse? That is what this is all about?" She turned to Bernard in disbelief. "This man sees a horse and you blame me?"

"Well, my lady, tis serious allegations made not just by Mr. Snape, but also a letter sent directly to me stating you were there."

Clarissa snorted. "Tis hearsay on both accounts."

"I saw your horse." Snape sneered.

"What time was this, Mr. Snape?"

"That evening, close to the house and around the time he was killed."

Clarissa stood up and took a turn around the room. "That's very interesting then."

"Why?" Bernard asked.

"Well, according to Mr. Snape, he was close enough to the house to see my horse."

"So?" Snape asked.

Clarissa faced Snape. "So, it also places you at Davenport's house at the time he was murdered."

Bernard shot a glance at Snape. "She has a point, Edmund. What were you doing there?"

Snape sputtered, "This is not about me. She was there. I saw her." He pointed his elongated, pointy finger at her.

Before Clarissa could answer, Dalziel appeared in the doorway and filled the room like a threatening presence and the edge to his voice was ice cold. "How dare you come into my home and question my wife in this manner?"

Snape paled. Bernard shifted uncomfortably in his seat.

Dalziel walked straight to Clarissa and pulled her into his side. It was a protective stance, one that spoke volumes to onlookers. "What is this about?"

"Beg your pardon me lord, but Mr. Snape here says he saw your wife's horse that night Lord Davenport was murdered. Someone also sent me a letter saying she caused his death. I am just enquiring."

Dalziel turned his gaze on Snape. "I would be very careful about making allegations against my wife."

Snape was about to say something when Dalziel asked, "Mr. Snape, you own lodgings near the Town Hall, am I correct?"

"Aye, but what has that—"

"And tis true you keep a mistress in that house while your wealthy wife whom you married for money lives three miles away oblivious to your extramarital affairs."

Snape appeared shocked and then outraged. "How dare you—"

Dalziel continued, "And not only is there a mistress, but you also have a young son there as well, do you not?"

Snape started sweating. "Are you threatening me?"

"Not at all. I'm merely wondering why you were near Davenport's house that night, which is three doors down from your mistress' house. Especially when you told your wife, who handles the purse strings, that you were away on business."

Snape went white as snow.

Then Dalziel moved in for the killer blow. "I looked into your affairs, Edmund, and I warned you to stay away from Clarissa. You refused. So, mark my words, I'm giving you a head start, to tell your wife the truth, because once I'm finished here, I will make an appointment to see her myself."

Snape did not say a word. He grabbed his hat, stood, and ran out of the room.

Clarissa stared in awe at her husband. She wondered how he became so astute and calculating. She was witnessing a master at play.

"Lord Stanhope, you are obstructing my enquiries!" Bernard sounded annoyed.

"Not when no crime has been committed by my wife."

"Tis my job to find out, not yours," Bernard declared.

"Then do your job, Bernard. How dare you come here with accusations and no solid proof!"

Bernard fished out a piece of paper from his leather boist. "Here, this letter arrived at my doorstep after Snape appeared with his testimony. It implicates the lady. I merely came to seek answers."

Dalziel took the letter and froze because it was signed by, *She-wolf*.

"Who sent this letter?" Dalziel demanded.

"I do not know. Twas slipped under my door while I was having breakfast," Bernard replied.

Clarissa was confused. When she read the letter over Dalziel's shoulder.

"You can tell this *She-wolf* liar that my wife was in bed with me that night, riding my cock and screaming in ecstasy… all night long," Dalziel growled.

Clarissa blushed bright red and pinched his arm to be quiet.

The shire-reeve looked extremely uncomfortable.

"And the next time you bring a serious accusation to my doorstep, you better make sure tis not a joke being played by bairns. Inspect the letter, you stupid man. Any fool can write this and send it."

Bernard read it again and looked embarrassed.

"I think tis time you left," Dalziel said.

Bernard nodded and took his leave.

"Why did you tell him we were making love that night?" Clarissa admonished.

"Because twas the truth. He will not pursue the matter if it's my word against his."

Clarissa collapsed into a chair. "I cannot make sense of why anyone would implicate me."

Dalziel clenched his jaw and said, "Tis personal, Love."

"What do you mean?"

"Ris, I think tis time we talked."

The Study, Stanhope

"WHAT DID YOU MEAN TIS personal? Who is this *She-wolf*?" Clarissa asked.

Dalziel sighed. "There are many secrets I must keep for the safety of others, but what I have to tell you is about your brother." Dalziel sat on the settee and pulled Clarissa into his arms, so she was on his lap. He held her tight. Preparing her for the news he had just received that afternoon.

Clarissa felt her heart beating faster the moment Dalziel mentioned Cedric. She was glad he held her close because, from his expression, she knew it was not good news.

"Go on," she rasped. Her voice breaking.

"I have reason to suspect Cedric is dead."

"What do you mean? How?" Clarissa was trembling and clutching his arms. A million thoughts flying through her head at once as waves of erratic emotions engulfed her from disbelief to grief to confusion. She felt a rising pit in her stomach and a hollowing out of her chest cavity, where she was sure her heart had stopped beating. Her breathing became shallow.

"Calm, Wife, shh... listen to me." Dalziel held her tighter and kept his gaze steady on her.

She was shaking, and the pain in her eyes shattered him. It was soul deep.

"Some weeks ago, Arrowsmith and I stopped at the town of *Dalmally* in Scotland. There we found the body of a man."

She clutched him tighter, then nodded as a signal to continue.

"They did not ken who he was, but I made a few inquiries since, and their shire-reeve got word to me today. He says the man was a *Bamburgh* local and known as 'Cedric'. There were body markings under his clothes."

"Wha... what were the markings?" she asked, with tears already streaming down her face. Clarissa held her breath and waited for his response.

"He had red hair, the scar of an old knife wound across his back, and a tattoo of an anchor on the right side of his chest."

Clarissa burst into tears and buried her head in Dalziel's shoulder because he had just described her brother. A guttural cry escaped her lips, "No, Cedric... no..."

Dalziel held Clarissa and rocked her in his arms and tried to absorb her pain. He felt as if his heart was breaking for her. He never said a word. Just let her grieve as he held her.

Eventually, the sobs ceased as she wiped her tears and nose with a handkerchief. She asked, "How? Why?"

"Tis believed your brother had information that got him killed."

She nodded and rested her head on his chest. Her heart was grief stricken. She and Cedric had been thick as thieves their whole life. He was her protective older brother, always providing for them when they had no one, and now she would have to carry on without him. Carry on their *Cause* without him.

"Do you ken why he was in *Dalmally*?" Dalziel asked.

She shook her head and sniffed. "There was no reason for him to be in Scotland at all. He stuck to the ports between here and France."

"Love, can you tell me what he did that took him away to France so often?"

Clarissa stiffened slightly, not knowing how much to say about Cedric's activities. But she knew she had to give him something.

She sat up and told him a half-truth. "Cedric was a kind soul, always trying to help people because..." She paused.

"Because?"

"We did not have the best upbringing. My mother was French, and my father was English. Twas an arranged marriage. She was very unhappy. There was little love between them and a lot of prejudice on both sides." She sniffed.

"Go on."

"My mother longed to return to France, but she never had the means and my father refused to let her see her family." Clarissa stared off into the distance. "He could be very cruel sometimes, and my mother faded away. Cedric wanted to help people like my mother, so he often traveled between the ports raising funds."

Clarissa cried again, and Dalziel left it at that. "But what does this have to do with *She-wolf*?" she asked between sobs.

It was Dalziel's turn to tell half-truths. "There have been a string of murders and beside the bodies, including your brother's, was a note written in French signed by someone calling themselves *She-wolf*. The notes have a perfumed fragrance, and they are intended for me."

Clarissa stared at him with concern. "Why you?"

"The king of Scotland has an assassin they call him *The Wolf*. I ken a little about him. This person sending the messages wants to show that they also ken who the Wolf is."

"What does this have to do with my brother?" Clarissa was confused.

"I believe Cedric may have also worked for my king and it got him killed."

Clarissa shook her head. "No, tis not possible, Cedric would never jeopardize the *safe*..." She paused.

"The safe what?"

"Nothing."

They were both quiet. Then a thought struck her. "Wait, I'll be right back." She leaped off his lap, then ran upstairs to her chambers. She retrieved the fragrant letter with the address on it, leaving the rest of the bundle in her drawer.

"What is this?" Dalziel asked when she returned and held it out to him.

"I found this in Davenport's desk the night he was killed. It has a fragrance to it."

Dalziel sniffed it and saw the handwriting. "Aye." He gritted his teeth. "Why did you not show me this before?"

"With everything that was happening, it just did not occur to me to share until now." She turned the letter over, pointing to the writing and asked, "Do you know what this means?"

Dalziel saw the words 'White Bear' and knew it referred to Earl Siward of Northumbria. Legend had it he was a descendant of a polar bear. Dalziel froze when he saw the *Glencoe* address at the top.

"Husband, do you ken who lives at that address? I think whoever it is, they killed Cedric," Clarissa said as fresh tears glistened in her eyes.

Dalziel nodded because he knew the occupant of that address. He had visited several times in the past. Dalziel got to work ensuring his household, and especially his wife, was well guarded against any attacks by *She-wolf*. Then he sent an urgent missive to Arrowsmith, notifying him that Lenora was their killer.

Berwick on Tweed, Northumbria

MILES AWAY IN A SMALL town called *Berwick upon Tweed*, Ewan Arrowsmith was sick of the stench of death and the treachery of men.

He just wanted to live a peaceful, uncomplicated life in the Highlands surrounded by family and friends and maybe a bonnie wife and bairns.

The face of a woman from his past flashed through his mind. *Beth.* How naïve he had been all those years ago to think she would have been happy to settle down with him. A poor farmer's son. He had not thought of her in years, yet here he was still trying to make something of himself and prove he was worthy of *her* when all she wanted was a nobleman. He gritted his teeth at the memory of her betrayal.

Beth was the reason Arrowsmith was now the King's Man in the North, stuck in a godforsaken country surrounded by godless men and death. *It was all her fault.* She was the reason his life went to shit. Arrowsmith brushed aside his maudlin thoughts and put her out of his mind. There was no use in rehashing the past. All it did was open old wounds, best left to scab over.

He trekked through the long grass to join the local shire-reeve and clenched his fists, his biggest concern now staring him dead in the face, literally. It was the body of a woman lying by the river. A perfumed letter was pinned to her expensive green cotton gown and surcoat. This time the message read, *"Comme on fait son lit, on se couche. Louve"*–*You've made your bed, now lie on it. She-wolf.*

He cursed the waste of a life cut off in its prime, and for what?

"Do you know this lady?" the shire-reeve asked.

"Aye, I ken who she is. My clerk will arrange the details of where to send the body."

If ever there was a sign that this was a personal vendetta against Dalziel, it was this. Arrowsmith took the note and placed it in his bag. He was about to leave when something caught his eye. It shimmered against the sunlight, though half of it was in the mud. He moved closer to take a better look. It was a necklace, a single gold chain. Arrowsmith stiffened. He had seen it before. He knew the owner. *But surely it couldn't be?*

He bent down and picked it up with a handkerchief, wrapped it, and placed it with the note.

Arrowsmith would have to proceed with caution. He would think on the chain later. For now, he needed to send a missive to Dalziel notifying him that his ex-mistress, Lenora, was the latest victim of *She-wolf.*

Driftwood Cottage, Bamburgh

THE DAY AFTER CLARISSA learned of Cedric's death, Dalziel escorted her to Driftwood Cottage so she could notify her family. Ruth and Martin took it the hardest, as they treated Cedric as a son. Ruth wailed in Martin's arms as the large man choked back sobs and fought back tears. Pierre and Jean-Luc allowed theirs to flow freely, as Cedric was like a brother to them.

Dalziel stood slightly apart, allowing them the privacy to mourn. He had found out the location where Cedric was buried so they could pay their respects in the future. He was grateful that his wife had a family who mourned with her. His one regret was he never got to meet Cedric. From the stories he heard, he knew he was a man of integrity with a great capacity to love. He had cared for and provided for his younger sister and his extended family and Dalziel was determined that Cedric's death and the secrets that caused it would not be in vain.

It had been an emotionally draining day for everyone, but Dalziel wanted nothing more than to remain by Clarissa's side. That night, they slept at the cottage surrounded by her family. Dalziel just held Clarissa as she cried herself to sleep.

Clarissa clung to her husband for support. He was her safe place to land when the world had just fallen out from under her. She realized then she loved him. The thought filled her with fear. *What if she lost him too?* Clarissa snuggled closer and felt him tighten his arms around her. She placed her cheek against his heart and allowed the steady sound of it beating, lull her to sleep.

Chapter 11 - Suspicion

My Beautiful Boy

Elspeth Davenport stared at the reflection glass and traced the lines of the scars across her stomach. It was something she did every morning to remind herself about the vicious nature of men and her resilience to survive. She bore the physical and mental battle scars of abuse and lived to tell the tale.

Elsa rejoiced when she heard the news of Davenport's death. A relief so profound settled over her being. Her only regret that she was not the one to bludgeon him to death. She knew it was wrong to think ill, of the dead, but in this case, she hoped his soul burned with everlasting torment for the pain he inflicted upon others.

As she dressed, she thought about her late husband and the life she had led under his rule. James Davenport was one of the meanest men she had ever known, and now she was free. Men like James were vile, and they twisted everything good in the world and made it feel evil. She recalled his false piety and talent for quoting biblical passages out of context to advance some twisted agenda.

His favorite passage to misquote was the one about wives submitting to their husbands. She knew it was a misquote because her mother had been part of the *Beguines* religious order. They were laywomen who knew their scriptures and, whilst they shunned many worldly desires; they turned no one away who needed their help. Elsa knew there was a second half to the passage rarely preached by men. That second part stated husbands were to love their wives as they would their own bodies. It was a two-way road. Something James conveniently ignored each time he beat her.

For such a publicly pious man, in private, he did everything to the contrary. Sexual immorality, impurity, idolatry, debauchery, he engaged in every kind of vice. Kept a string of mistresses under their roof, but heaven forbid she called him on it. She would pay physically. Elsa abhorred that type of life and would never accept it. Vows made before God were sacred, yet he broke every single one. She gritted her teeth, bitter and angry that his fine eyes and fake promises duped her.

Elsa cast her mind back to another time, when she had a good man by her side who loved her, cherished, and protected her and wanted the best for her. But that was not meant to be.

Unforeseen circumstances had caused her hasty marriage to Davenport, and Elsa had regretted it ever since. It would have been better for her to live as an outcast than the seven years she endured under his roof. He had lauded her secret over her for years to keep her compliant and, in his twisted way, ensured she suffered for it. He sent Jordan, her precious son, away to a monastery at five years of age, then threatened her daily that if she did not comply with his wishes, something untoward would happen to him.

But all that was about to change. Thanks to Clarissa. Elsa finally had access to her son and for the first time in two years, she was going to see him again.

Three hours later, Elsa was in the town of *Alnwick* in Northumbria, sitting in the office of an abbot awaiting Jordie's arrival. Jean-Luc stood beside her, providing welcome support for her nerves. He had been a rock for her during her entire ordeal and she only hoped he was not forming a tendre for her because she already knew she would never enter a loveless marriage again.

"Mrs. Davenport, I am extremely sorry for your loss. I have arranged everything so Jordan can be placed in your tender care. No doubt he needs a parent close by now that his father has passed," the abbot said.

"Thank you, Abbot Cullen, for your kindness. I know he would appreciate coming home with me for a short period of mourning, at least until he adjusts to his loss." Elsa crossed her fingers in her lap. It was a lie; she was never bringing her son back. Once they left, they were both going to disappear off the face of the earth and never return.

"Well, he is a pleasant young man, and I am sure you will both benefit from time together. Just as a matter of precaution, I need to sight the Will and letters and he can return home with you."

"Of course." Elsa opened her reticule and pulled out the parchments for him to sight. She and Jean-Luc were then ushered into a smaller room to await her son.

Elsa was nervous. It has been two years since she had seen Jordan. She cried for weeks when James cut off all access. She only hoped Jordie still remembered her.

She was just telling Jean-Luc how impatient she was to see Jordie when she heard running footsteps in the hall and someone yell, "Master Jordan, do not run!" The sound ricocheted across the vacuous hallway. No sooner were those words uttered when the door to the room burst wide open. Before Clarissa could catch her breath, a bundle of gangly limbs, dark brown hair, and hazel eyes came barreling towards her. Clarissa stood and had just enough time to brace herself before his head hit her stomach and his arms banded around her waist. "Mama!" Jordie cried. "Mama, I knew you would come for me. I knew you had not forgotten me."

She wrapped her arms around her boy, stroked his hair, and bent down to kiss his cheek. "Jordie, my beautiful boy... my beautiful, beautiful boy." Elsa cried with happiness.

Jean-Luc interrupted their reunion. "We need to go tis getting late," he whispered.

Ten minutes later, they were on their way back to the safety of the *cove* and the *safe house*. This time Elsa's joy was complete because she held the world in her arms.

⁂

Dis-Harmony

"NO. NO. NO! YOU LIE... you lie!" Harmony Durham screamed after hearing the news of Cedric's death. She picked up a vase and threw it across the drawing room of her town house. It shattered across the fireplace and Lily, her kitten, ran out of the room. Harmony then stormed about the room, kicking inanimate objects in her path and swiping items off tables. In between bouts of crying and ranting incoherently.

"Harmony, please calm down," Clarissa said. Maintaining a safe distance.

Pierre was currently trying to remove the shattered remnants of the vase to prevent anyone from stepping on the pieces.

Clarissa and Pierre had stopped in to see Harmony and notify her of Cedric's death.

The visit was not going well.

"*Mademoiselle*, be careful. You will hurt yourself." Pierre was already across the room, his arms banded around a struggling Harmony who was trying to break free so she could smash the window with a fire poker.

Realizing she could not get out of his hold, she crumpled onto the floor, taking Pierre down with her. Then she wailed and clung to Pierre as he held her and quietly soothed her in French.

Clarissa felt the wet hit her eyes again. She did not know Harmony felt so deeply for Cedric. Her grief deepened.

"We were going to marry," Harmony kept repeating as she wept.

"Shh... you will be all right, *mademoiselle*." Pierre consoled her.

"If there is anything you need, you only have to ask, and we will be here for you." Clarissa was now on the floor, sitting beside the two of them.

Harmony just nodded and continued to weep.

Goldie

AN HOUR LATER, CLARISSA and Pierre left Harmony to the care of her servants. It had been a difficult day, and Clarissa needed to keep her mind occupied with other things.

After running several errands with Pierre, they headed to the *cove* and the *safe house*. The women and children were away for the day, so it would provide her some quiet time to catch up on correspondence. She was just approaching the front door when Pierre pulled her back and pushed her behind him.

"What the—"

He shuffled them back against the wall and signaled for her to be quiet.

Clarissa was trying to figure out what was happening when he pointed to the front door.

It was then she noticed the broken lock.

"Stay here," Pierre demanded.

She tried to stop him from leaving, but he was already ducking and moving around to the back entrance, keeping clear of the windows.

Clarissa waited for what felt like hours, but she knew could only be several minutes.

She was about to go in search when she heard a scuffling sound from inside the house and things crashing, then Pierre's voice yelling, "Run, Ris... run!"

She heard a thud, and he went silent.

Clarissa peered inside the window and paled. Pierre was slumped over on the ground and her worst nightmare stood beside him. He was unmistakable to miss with his bald head, gold teeth, and tattoos from the top of his head to his fingertips. It was Goldie, the owner of the brothel and the docks.

He had two large men with him. They all turned to the window and saw her. "Get her, she comes wiv us," Goldie commanded and signaled to his men.

Clarissa turned on her heel and ran up the steep path and straight into the woods. She knew the *cove* like the back of her hand and all its hiding places. She just needed to get to the cliff-top. There was a hidden passage that led down to the caves. It was her only chance to lose them. Adrenalin pumping through her veins. Her speed increased. Clarissa could hear the men hot on her tail as they came crashing through the forest. They were gaining on her and her panic was escalating. She stumbled and fell, and as she was trying to rise, a man grabbed her ankle. She kicked him in the face, scrambled away, and kept running.

"You bitch," he shouted.

Clarissa headed straight into the thickets and kept moving. They closed behind her as she pushed forward. She broke through into the clearing and headed straight for the edge of the large flat rock overlooking the ocean. Clarissa realized she was too late because another man was now a few yards away from her. She turned to face him.

"Come ere lass, tis better if ye dint struggle."

She shook her head. 'Never." Clarissa inched backward towards the cliff's edge.

He tried to grab her. At the last minute, she shifted to her right, and he propelled past her and over the edge, plunging to his death.

A second man came crashing through the thickets to her left side, catching her off guard. He grabbed her by the arm and overpowered her. Clarissa knew she was in trouble. No one knew where she was, and this did not bode well for her. Sheer panic and adrenalin kicked in, and she started punching and kicking to get free.

He slapped her across the face. "Stop it."

Clarissa head-butted him when he moved in closer. He yelped in pain as blood streamed from his nose. Then he backhanded her, threw her onto the ground, and straddled her.

"Tis a pity for ye, Goldie does not care what condition I return ye." He laughed.

Clarissa fought him off as best she could, even as his hands tore at her dress. She tried to find a weapon, anything, a rock, something she could hit him with. She was grasping at anything she could find on the ground when an arrow lodged in her attacker's throat.

Blood spurted out from his neck and showered her with droplets. She covered her face. He held onto his neck, gurgled, then toppled sideways, freeing her.

Clarissa rolled onto her feet in time to watch Arrowsmith step out from the copse of trees. Quiver of arrows strapped to his back, a bow in his hand. He walked directly to her and asked, "Are you all right?"

"Yes," she replied, her voice wavering.

Arrowsmith grunted, then took her hand and led them back towards the house. He did not say a word.

Clarissa followed in silence. Her dress was torn, blood splattered across her face, her hair had escaped its bun and she was trying to calm her nerves.

By the time they arrived at the *safe house*, it was quiet. Arrowsmith ushered her into the hallway. "Dinnae look at him," he said, and blocked her view of the body lying there.

She could not help herself as she peeked around him. She glimpsed Goldie slumped over in the hallway, an arrow sticking out of his right eye socket.

Arrowsmith took her to Pierre, who was nursing a lump on his forehead but was otherwise all right.

She let go of Arrowsmith's hand and ran to crouch down beside him.

"What happened?" she finally asked.

Pierre said, "Goldie was searching for Sally Greene and you. He said someone paid handsomely for you."

Clarissa shuddered. "What does that mean?"

"It means you've made some powerful enemies, Lady Stanhope," Arrowsmith drawled from behind her as he brought her a wet cloth to wipe the blood from her face.

"Twas fortunate the house was empty, or he might have killed everyone. If not for Mr. Arrowsmith here, I'd be dead too," Pierre said.

Clarissa stood, wiping her face, and thanked Arrowsmith for saving them.

Arrowsmith said nothing, his face still a mask of indifference.

"Will you tell my husband about this?" she asked with uncertainty.

"With the bruises forming on your face and the way ye look right now, I dinnae think it will be easy to keep any of this from him," Arrowsmith replied.

Pierre then asked Arrowsmith, "What exactly were you doing out here? Tis a secret location."

"If ye must ken, I was following Goldie. I didna have any notion he would bring me to you." He gave Clarissa a quelling stare. "I'll have the bodies taken care of," Arrowsmith said before he turned to go.

Clarissa panicked. She called out, "Mr. Arrowsmith, I... please do not tell Dalziel."

Arrowsmith turned around and replied, "You need to tell him yourself about who you are, where you go, and what you get up to down at the *cove*."

"Have you been spying on me?" She got her back up.

"Aye, I have been keeping watch, but today I found out more than you could ever imagine."

"Twas you who told my husband I was with a French man. That's why he came home angry from Scotland." She accused.

"Aye, I did."

"Why did you not just ask me?" Clarissa asked.

Arrowsmith replied, "Because I dinnae trust you. You keep so many secrets from him."

"That is between Dalziel and me. I'll not have you interfere." Clarissa was getting angry.

Arrowsmith walked straight up to her and said, "He deserves a woman who doesna lie to him."

"What did you say?" She felt affronted.

"You heard me loud and clear, Lady Stanhope."

They stared at each other in stony silence, then Arrowsmith said, "Dalziel and I, we work in a world filled with people who have nothing but treachery and deceit in their hearts. The *one* safe place for us is our homes."

"I do not understand why that has anything to do with me?" Clarissa snapped.

Arrowsmith clenched his jaw. "You lead him on a merry dance, even in his own home."

"I am not leading him on a—"

"Aye, you do. The secret outings at night, the lies about your movements. What do you call that?"

Clarissa blushed and said defensively, "I cannot tell him. There are bigger matters at play you could not possibly understand."

"I may not, but you need to trust that Dalziel will. The more he kens, the better he can protect you and himself."

They stood in silence for several moments before Arrowsmith said, "Tell him the truth. He deserves a woman he can trust and a home that is safe. Do it before tis too late."

With those words, Arrowsmith walked out of the room.

Stanhope Estate, Bamburgh

DALZIEL RETURNED HOME to find Clarissa absent. He retreated to his study and cleared some correspondence. On top of a pile was a missive from Arrowsmith. Judging by the date stamp, it arrived the day before, which he had missed. When he opened it, he stilled. *Lenora was dead?* He scanned the contents and gritted his teeth in frustration. No wonder his men could not find her.

"Blast it!" he cursed and paced, wondering who the hell *She-wolf* was and why Lenora of all people was now a victim.

He went through more correspondence when Mrs. Armstrong interrupted him.

"Me lord, this came just now. Twas sitting on the outside landing." She handed him a folded note, then walked out again.

There was no address, but the words he read saw him seeing red.

"Lady Stanhope is frolicking at the cove with unscrupulous men. Mayhap you should keep a closer eye lest your heir resemble Mr. Arrowsmith."

Dalziel screwed the note up in his hand and threw it in the fire. Then he waited for his wife to return.

Clarissa entered the house just before suppertime. She had cleaned herself up the best she could and tried to cover over the bruising so as not to upset her husband. She went in search of him and found him sitting by the fireplace, drinking. He did not move or stand to greet her as he usually did.

"Dalziel? Are you all right?"

"What were you doing down at the cove?" he asked, still staring at the flames.

"Did Arrowsmith tell you?"

Dalziel glared at her. Already the jealous machinations burning through his brain. "So tis true then?" He turned to face her, then faltered when he saw the state of her. "What the devil happened to you?" He was up off the seat and by her side in seconds.

"It happened at the cove I wa—"

"Did Arrowsmith hit you?" he roared.

"No! Twas, not him. If you would just calm down."

"Is Arrowsmith your lover?" He gritted his teeth.

"Are you daft?" Clarissa recoiled at his accusation. "Of course not. He saved my life."

"What do you mean?"

"Someone tried to attack me at the cove, and Arrowsmith stepped in."

"Who tried to attack you?"

"I cannot tell you."

He stared at her for a moment, made an exasperated sound, then asked, "Are you all right?" He looked her over, checking for injuries.

"Yes, I am fine."

He picked her up in his arms and headed for their chambers. He was calling orders for the servants to draw a bath and bring food.

"Dalziel. I am fine. Stop shouting and put me down."

He ignored her and kept walking up the stairs.

When they were in his chambers, he started acting as lady's maid as servants arrived to fill the tub with boiling water.

Dalziel's mind was in disarray. Part jealousy and uncertainty, but mostly a concern for his wife. She appeared a mess with bruises scattered across her otherwise flawless skin.

When she was bathed and dressed, he felt calm enough to ask her again.

"Why were you at the cove and who attacked you?"

"I cannot tell you, Husband. I'm sorry."

Dalziel silently studied her for the longest time as she appeared contrite.

"You cannot or will not tell me?"

"Both, I am sorry."

"Even something as important as this?" His expression was incredulous.

She shook her head.

"Right. Have at it, love." He stood and started gathering his things.

"What do you mean? Where are you going?"

"I am done," he replied.

"What do you mean, you're done?"

"Exactly what it means. You will not tell me anything. You disappear for hours, come back with bruises, go to god kens where at nights and give me... *nothing!*" he roared the last word.

With that, he walked out of the room.

Clarissa followed behind, begging for him to trust her. Dalziel ignored her, walked into his study, slammed the door shut, and locked it.

He slept in a spare room that night while Clarissa waited for him to come to bed.

That was the beginning of the end.

All the King's Men

THE FOLLOWING MORNING, Dalziel paid a surprise visit to Arrowsmith. He needed to know what happened at the cove, and he needed to know whether he could trust him.

It was still early, so he banged his fist on the door.

Instead of a butler or a maid answering, a disheveled and shirtless Arrowsmith answered the door as if just roused from sleep. He grunted and let Dalziel inside.

Dalziel immediately recognized he had interrupted Arrowsmith and a lover when he heard a woman's voice call out from somewhere in the large house, "Who is it?"

"No one," Arrowsmith yelled over his shoulder, then grimaced.

"I am sorry to interrupt. I can come back another time." Dalziel was about to go.

"No, tis all right. She needs to leave, wait." Arrowsmith disappeared down the hallway.

Dalziel heard murmurs, then arguing, then shouting, mainly from the woman in question. Then he heard her cursing, stomping footsteps, and a backdoor slam.

Arrowsmith returned soon after, looking fresher with a white leine on and his long hair tied back.

"You did not need to chase her out on my account," Dalziel said.

"Believe me, I did. I dinnae ken why she was still here this morning. It irritates me when she does that."

"Is she local?"

"Aye, and getting a little too close for comfort," Arrowsmith replied.

Dalziel raised a brow. "If your intentions are not serious, let her ken the way of it and perhaps end it."

"I have tried. She is none too bright," he replied, then dismissed the subject.

They moved into a large study, and he ushered Dalziel to sit.

"We have a lot to discuss," Dalziel said.

"Aye, we do." Arrowsmith agreed.

By the end of their lengthy meeting, Dalziel discovered Goldie had attacked Clarissa, and Pierre and Arrowsmith protected her.

He shuddered to think what would have happened if they had not been there.

Arrowsmith assured him that contrary to what the note said, he was not Clarissa's lover, nor would he ever dally with a married woman.

That eased Dalziel's jealousy but caused greater concern. Someone was following Clarissa and sending these notes. He was going to put a stop to all her activities from now on.

Both men shared what they had found of Elspeth Davenport's whereabouts. Arrowsmith believed she could still be hiding locally while Dalziel would continue searching for her further afield.

Elspeth was the missing key. It was rumored Lord Davenport's list had names and dates for future attacks on Scotland and the names of Earl Siward's informants in Scotland. Elsa had stolen the list when she ran away as surety.

The problem was, according to Arrowsmith, it just made her a target for the powerful men on the list. Dalziel knew time was running out to protect the woman and get her to Macbeth.

With Davenport's death, messages were still filtering to Siward. Both men suspected Lancet and Chamberlain most likely murdered their friend.

They agreed to maintain their vigilance over the 'The Three Lords' club.

They also discussed Lenora's death and tried to discover how she was linked to the other murders, including Cedric's. As for the identity of *She-wolf*, they came up empty-handed.

Whilst they were talking, Dalziel noticed Arrowsmith appeared hesitant.

"Spit it out. Whatever you are holding back, say it," Dalziel said.

"I dinnae ken how to broach this topic," Arrowsmith replied.

"Why dinnae you just say it and we can go from there?"

Arrowsmith poured them a drink and shoved one towards Dalziel. Dalziel refused. "Tis too early."

"Take it. I ken you are going to need it once I finish saying what I'm about to say."

Dalziel accepted it and braced. "Go on."

Arrowsmith moved across the room, retrieved something from a draw, and placed it in front of Dalziel.

"Why are you showing me a dirty chain?"

"Look closer. Does it seem familiar?"

"It's Clarissa's." Dalziel seemed confused.

"Aye, and it was next to Lenora's body in the mud."

Dalziel felt tension rip through his spine. "What are you suggesting?"

"Nothing at this stage, not from the chain alone, but..."

"But what?" Dalziel's entire body was rigid.

"If you piece several things together, it forms a different picture." Arrowsmith took a deep breath. "Just hear me out. Your wife, how much do you really ken about her?"

"Enough to ken she is not involved." Dalziel knew he was lying. Clarissa never gave him her whole truth, and neither did he, but her secrets were extensive.

"Do you not think tis a coincidence that the one person connected to every aspect of these murders is your wife?" Arrowsmith asked.

"No, I dinnae believe it, she would not play me false—"

"She is part, French. The letters are written in French. Her brother was an informant for Macbeth and went missing when he had news about Siward's movements. She was there in the house when Davenport was killed, she retrieved a Will and letters from his office she kenned her way around his library. You told me yourself."

Dalziel nodded.

"She mysteriously found a perfumed letter in a drawer. I found her gold chain near Lenora's body. She roams the taverns and docks at night, she is kenned by Goldie of all people."

"Are you implying my wife is, '*She-wolf*'? Surely, she would not kill her own brother?" Dalziel said in disbelief.

"With the right incentive, a killer will do anything. Whoever kens you are the *Wolf*, would ken how to manipulate your life."

"I refuse to believe the worst of her." Dalziel shook his head.

"Rationalize and separate, never get attached. That is the rule we live by Dalziel. Dinnae let your guard down, not even for a bonnie wife."

Dalziel picked up his glass of whiskey and downed the contents. Arrowsmith was right, he needed that drink. As much as he wanted to reject the idea, it already planted seeds of doubt as darkness descended over Dalziel. An internal war raged within him. If Clarissa were involved, he would have to hand her over to Macbeth and there was no way he could do that. Not even for his king.

Dalziel would need to distance himself from her. He needed to prepare in case she turned out to be a liar and deadly murderess.

Chapter 12 – Ending Things

Moving Out

Clarissa sensed subtle changes about her husband since that night at the cove. Gone was the easy banter they once shared and the occasional smiles. Instead, he became quiet and broody. He watched her every move and often they would sit in an uncomfortable silence during meals for long periods.

Clarissa felt adrift. She missed her husband; she missed him in her bed; she missed talking to him at breakfast.

Clarissa attempted to initiate conversation. "I think we should talk, husband."

"Aye, we do. From now on, I dinnae want you near the docks or running about the countryside alone. I have organized two men to follow you everywhere. I should have done it sooner."

"Tis unnecessary, Husband."

"Tis not a negotiation, Wife. Now, I am going out and I expect you not to court trouble." He stood up and left without another word.

Clarissa felt a sense of foreboding. He was not even going to listen to her.

That night Clarissa waited up for Dalziel again, and it was the first time he did not come home at all. She was frantic with worry, only to see him stumble in the next morning. He did not speak to her or say a word. He merely went up to his chamber, locked the door, and slept.

This went on for three days. Eventually, Clarissa cornered him on his way to his study. He feigned he was busy and shut the door. She knew then he was shutting her out completely.

Clarissa did the only thing she could. She threw herself into her work at the *safe house* and increasingly spent more time at Driftwood Cottage with Ruth and Martin.

By the end of the week, she packed some of her belongings and moved into the *safe house*. It made more sense for her to remain there rather than travel back and forth between the *cove*, the cottage, and the estate. Clarissa also slipped past Dalziel's guards on more than one occasion, but otherwise, she did not mind them being close by. It was an added security measure, although she never led them to the cove. Clarissa doubted Dalziel would even notice she was no longer at Stanhope.

IT HAD BEEN A WEEK since Dalziel had seen his wife, and he missed her. He had purposefully timed his arrivals and departures during times he knew she would be out or sleeping. But he needed to keep his wits about him. He assumed she was in her rooms.

He was currently sleeping in a spare bedroom at Arrowsmith's house on a lumpy bed. Arrowsmith was mostly away, so he was not underfoot.

It had to end. He decided he would attempt to spend time with Clarissa. Maybe if he could gain her trust, she would open up to him.

Dalziel went home and stayed put. He was looking forward to supper when he would finally see his wife. When supper came around, he asked Mr. Bell where Clarissa was.

"She is not in, my lord."

"Well, where is she?"

"She has not been home all week."

He paused, his glass midway to his lips. "What do you mean, she has not been home all week?"

Mrs. Armstrong appeared with a large crockery pot and ladle. She placed it in front of him.

"I believe, me lord, the mistress has moved out because *someone* has been neglecting her," Mrs. Armstrong snapped.

"What? When?"

"Oh, a few days now," a maid replied.

"And no one thought to tell me?" He scowled.

"Well, ye were never home, and I doubt ye would have noticed, even if ye were." Mrs. Armstrong shrugged her shoulders.

Dalziel stood and marched out of the room. "Ready my horse. I am going to fetch my bloody wife." He was irate.

"If you're thinking of heading to the cottage, she is not there either," Mr. Bell said.

He stopped to ask, "Then where the bloody hell is she?"

Mr. Bell just shrugged.

Ten minutes later, Dalziel was grilling the two men who guarded her. "Where is my wife?"

"We are not sure."

"What do you mean, you are not sure?" He clenched his fists, annoyed with the English guards he had hired.

"Tis difficult to keep up, she gives us the slip a lot."

"Are you telling me you dinnae ken where she goes at night?"

They both nodded.

"What the bloody hell am I paying you for?" Dalziel asked.

"Me lord, she's very good at escaping."

Dalziel could only think of one place he had never been. *The Cove.*

And so it was *the Wolf,* rode out into the dark night. He was in a feral mood. No longer a gentleman, but a rabid beast. He was an assassin. He could track anyone's movements and sneak up on them wherever they were and yet, for the life of him, he could not even find his blasted wife.

An hour later, he stood outside a large rock-hewn house built within the cove. *How could he know so little about her?* Was she a paramour to a wealthy man? He clenched his fists.

"So ye finally showed. Tis about time," Martin said.

"What are you doing here, Martin?"

"I am guarding the house. And I suggest if you're here to cause my mistress trouble, then ye better move on."

"What is this place?" Dalziel asked.

"Mayhap you need to inquire with your wife. She runs it."

"She runs this place?"

"Aye," Martin replied.

Before he knew it, Dalziel's feet were moving towards the door. Then he was inside the hallway. He followed the sound of children's laughter and stood outside a large room with a vast fireplace.

Five children gathered around Clarissa as she animatedly told them a story, making up the voices of the characters. She was laughing with a sparkle in her eyes.

Dalziel smiled at the sight. She was lovely, and he missed her.

Clarissa raised her head, and that alerted the others to his presence. Dalziel felt a tension sweep across the room as everyone went quiet. It was then he understood the feeling. It was *fear*, and he felt it tenfold. The women and children *feared* him.

He stepped away from the door and gently said to Clarissa, "I just came to make sure you were well. We will talk at home."

Clarissa missed her husband so much and seeing him here now filled her aching heart. But she saw something in his eyes... sadness. Clarissa knew there would be many questions to answer now that he knew about the *cove*, but now was not the time to talk. She nodded in acknowledgment and continued telling the story to the children. She felt the tension in the room ease when Dalziel left.

Dalziel returned home, a hollow ache in his chest. He knew then the woman in that room was not capable of murder. Whatever was going on with her life, she was not *She-wolf.* His instincts had never been wrong.

What saddened Dalziel, though, was that he really knew nothing of her life outside of Stanhope. Too many secrets existed between them, and he wondered if she would ever open up to him. He had so many things he wanted to ask, but now was not the time. He would give her time to trust him and tell him everything in good time.

IT HAD BEEN A DAY SINCE he had seen Clarissa at the cove and Dalziel was furious because the blasted woman had still not come home or told him anything. His blood boiled over. If he were a vampire, he was sure he would have exploded in the sunlight by now. His patience was wearing thin. Waiting around for his wife to come to him was torture. The longer he waited, the angrier he became. As a result, he became increasingly annoyed and, for the first time in his life, Dalziel *sulked*.

The List

CLARISSA WAS BAKING bread in the kitchen at the *safe house* when Elsa and Jean-Luc appeared. She invited them to sit and take some tea and biscuits.

She put the bread in the wood fire oven and joined them.

"Is everything all right?"

"We have a problem Ris. I cannot take Elsa and Jordie to France," Jean-Luc said.

"Why not? I already booked passage."

"Elsa has something she needs to do first, and we need your help."

"What do you need to do?" Clarissa asked Elsa.

"There are people after this list." Elsa took out a parchment from her reticule.

Clarissa glanced at it with confusion when Elsa handed her the piece of vellum.

"Siward, the Earl of Northumbria, trusted my late husband with this list. These are the dates and names of places he will attack in Scotland. He wants to kill King Macbeth."

Clarissa gasped in surprise and dropped the list on the table as if it were hot coal.

Elsa picked up the list and pointed at the second column. "And these are the names of Siward's contacts in Scotland."

Clarissa paled. "Who knows, you have this?"

"Men, he did business with Chamberlain and Lancet. I think they murdered him for this list.

"But why?"

"Siward wants to dethrone Macbeth to claim Scotland for Malcolm of Cranmore. Macbeth and Malcolm are related. There has been rivalry among their families for years," Elsa replied.

"What has any of this got to do with you?" Clarissa asked.

"Chamberlain and Lancet want to use this list to make a deal with Macbeth against Malcolm. I do not know why, I only overhead an argument between them and James. I knew it must be important for them to fight over it."

"But why do you have it?" Clarissa asked.

"I took it to protect myself. I told Davenport if he tried to find me, I would divulge the contents of the list."

"Why are you telling me this?" Clarissa asked.

"Because I want Earl Siward to pay. He arranged my marriage and now I have heard he and my late husband have men out searching for me." Elsa had an angry glint in her eyes.

"I am sorry for what you endured Elsa, truly I am, but this is beyond me. I do not know what you want me to do with this."

Elsa asked, "Your husband is a Scottish thane, is he not?"

"Yes," Clarissa said warily.

"I was hoping he could take this list to his king."

Clarissa inhaled a deep breath. She was not even sure if she trusted her husband enough to ask him, but she knew he worked for the Scottish king in some capacity.

"You place a lot of trust in my husband, Elsa. What if it all goes wrong?"

"Tis a risk I will take because the longer I hold on to it, the more people will try to find me and Jordie."

"All right, I will see what I can do."

Clarissa thought more about their predicament. She knew she was going to have to tell Dalziel the whole truth. It was time she trusted her husband. It was the only way to keep them all safe.

But things were about to change in a matter of hours.

The Whole Truth

CLARISSA RETURNED HOME to speak to Dalziel. She was nervous, but it was necessary. She admitted she had been hiding away; it was time to overcome her uncertainty and trust him.

Mrs. Armstrong was happy to see her and told her Dalziel was in the library. Clarissa hovered on the threshold, took a deep breath, then walked in.

Dalziel was stretched out on the long settee, reading a book.

"I need to speak to you, Husband. Tis most urgent."

He looked up and stilled for a moment, then his face was a mask of indifference as he returned to the book he was reading.

"Then have at it," he replied coldly. But did not meet her eyes again.

Clarissa moved closer. She could hear him flipping his pages nonchalantly, as if he were still reading.

She stopped in front of him and waited as he kept reading.

"Well, spit it out. Why have you interrupted my quiet time?" he grumbled.

"I need to..." She wrung her hands, feeling nervous, and it was not helping that he was acting so coldly towards her.

"Say it, woman, I have to go out tonight." He flipped more pages.

"Where are you going?" She frowned.

"I believe where I go at nights is none of your concern, seeing as you tell me nothing about your movements."

Clarissa felt a streak of jealousy. "Do you have a lover? Need I remind you, Husband, we made marriage vows."

Dalziel met her eyes for the first time and stated, "If I had a lover, twould be none of your concern because need I remind *you*, Wife, a man can do whatever he bloody well likes."

If he had struck her in the face, it would have been less painful. She inhaled sharply. Clarissa realized whatever she had to say was pointless. She had left it too late, just as Arrowsmith had warned.

Deflated, she beat a hasty retreat. "I see. I... I'm sorry I bothered you," she whispered. Stung by the rejection and mortified by the implication she no longer mattered to him, Clarissa spun around and ran for the door. She could feel wet running down her cheek from tears she could not control and cursed herself for the unwanted display of emotion.

Clarissa turned the door handle and was pulling the door open when she felt Dalziel behind her. His hand pushed it shut again. She remained still, facing the door, Dalziel's front pressed against her back, trapping her in place. How he had moved across the room so quietly she would never know.

She could feel his heat against her. This was the closest they had been in days. Clarissa felt his breath at her nape and his lips against her ear.

"I'm sorry, Love. There is no one else. Please stay and talk to me."

She turned around to face him, their lips inches apart. Her back was against the door and Dalziel had moved closer, crowding her body with his.

He stared into her eyes, and she saw it then, vulnerability and sadness. His eyes reflected her own.

Dalziel noticed the sheen of tears and said, "Dinnae cry Love, please, I cannot bear it." He leaned forward and kissed her cheek, then wiped a tear away with his thumb.

"Tell me what ye wanted to say." He moved away from her, clasped her hand in his, and walked her back to the settee. When she went to sit, he sat first and pulled her onto his lap.

Clarissa could not help her reaction. She leaned forward and gently kissed his lips. "I am sorry, Husband. There is much I must tell you and not all of it you will like."

Dalziel nodded but continued to hold her. He was happy to have her in his arms again, and finally, she was going to trust him enough to tell him the truth.

He took a deep breath and said, "Tell me."

"You need to promise me you will not get angry, but hear me out, please?"

"Aye, but if—"

She placed a finger on his lips. "No buts. Just nod your head and agree."

He grinned for the first time. "Aye, go on."

"I run a haven for women who are hiding from violent men. Some of these men are powerful, titled. I keep these women safe in the house at the cove that you saw. We, that is, Cedric, my cousins, and I, provide them and their children shelter until we can move them to a more permanent home."

"I see. Please continue," he said.

"Before I tell you anymore, I need to explain why I have kept these things from you."

"All right Love, tell me." He kissed the tip of her nose.

She took a deep breath and absentmindedly ran her fingers along the collar of his leine. "My parents wed under an arranged marriage. My father was a debt-ridden English man with a title, and my mother was the daughter of a wealthy French merchant who coveted an English title."

"What happened to them?"

"They were miserable. It was not a love match, and my father gambled away most of my mother's fortune. He was a violent, volatile man when he was in his cups and abused her regularly."

Dalziel clenched his jaw as he listened. But he wished if Clarissa's father were there, he would have bashed him to death.

"What happened to your ma, sweeting?"

"Mother tried to leave him, to return to France, but my father would not let her go. One night, she escaped with us. She planned it for several months. My aunt sent her funds to escape. We got as far as *Pas de Calais*, the Dover Narrows."

"And then?"

"My father was waiting for us there."

"But how did he ken?"

"Mother made the mistake of telling one of her friends who was married to a powerful nobleman. Her friend let it slip and her husband notified my father. He thought it morally reprehensible that a lady should leave her husband."

"Bloody fool. What happened then?" Dalziel asked, although he suspected he knew the answer.

"When we returned home, my father was so angry that my mother had humiliated him in front of his peers. He beat her to death. The nobles acted as if nothing happened. They said it was his right to do as he pleased with his wife."

"I am so sorry, Love."

Clarissa lay her head on his shoulder. "If my mother had a safe place to go, she would not have died that night. I can only imagine the pain and fear she must have lived with," Clarissa said in a raspy whisper.

Dalziel held her tighter. "Aye."

"Cedric and I, after what happened, we vowed to help other women who had no one they could trust. So, we built the house on the cove. Soon, word spread about our *Cause*."

"Who are the women you take in?" Dalziel asked.

Clarissa sat up straighter. "Prostitutes, wives, maids, mistresses, paramours. Cedric made sure we always had enough funds to feed everyone, even if sometimes we..."

"You what?"

"Smuggled goods to and from France."

"That's why Cedric traveled along the ports?"

"Yes."

Dalziel just stared at his wife in awe. *This* was her big secret. That she was helping women and children. Then the gravity of what she was telling him sunk in. By taking on this role, Clarissa made herself a target of powerful, titled men.

"Do you realize you put your life in danger with this endeavor?" he said.

"Yes, but tis worth the risk."

Dalziel glared at her. "You are not worth the risk!"

"Do you ever think about the plight of these women at all?" She implored.

"No, because I have many things on my mind, one of which is to protect my wife."

"But what of the others? The women who have no other choice but to sell their bodies, be they prostitutes, or mistresses, and I'll even say it... wives?"

Dalziel flinched at the word, knowing theirs had started as a simple arrangement for the exchange of money. No, he was not like any of the men she bundled him with.

Dalziel asked, "What of their husbands? You make powerful enemies of them all."

"Only if they find out who I am."

Dalziel gritted his teeth. He knew she had a point, but he could still see so many pitfalls and holes in her strategy, each one leading her down a dangerous path.

"I still dinnae like the thought of you putting yourself in danger," he replied.

"Danger faces all women in this world, husband especially when they have nowhere to go. Do you ever think about what happens to women once their husbands, lovers, protectors, employers have discarded them?" She raised her brow.

Dalziel was quiet.

"And are you still a smuggler?" he snapped and clenched his jaw.

Now Clarissa was indignant. "Do not judge me, Husband. Smuggling kept us afloat these past five years."

"Tis also a bloody dangerous past-time. No wonder you attracted the ire of Goldie and the shire-reeve. Who kens what other men you have pissed off with your activities?"

She just glared at him.

"So, this is your secret."

She nodded her head.

"Why did you think you could not trust me before?" he asked.

"Because you are a wealthy, titled man and at any moment you could have turned us all in," she replied.

He paused and thought that through and finally saw things from her perspective.

"Well, starting tomorrow, things are going to change."

Clarissa tensed. "What do you mean?"

"I mean, tis time you had proper help. If Goldie and his men found you easily, many men could venture to the cove and it would leave you vulnerable."

"You will help me?" she asked in awe.

"Of course, I will help you. How else am I going to protect my own damned woman?"

Clarissa sighed and decided it was time to tell him the whole truth. "There is one more thing."

He raised an eyebrow. She took that as her cue to continue.

"One woman I have been hiding is Lord Davenport's widow and her son."

Dalziel froze. He felt a tingle up his spine. "What did you just say?"

"I have been hiding Elsa Davenport and her son and now Siward, the Earl of Northumbria, is after her and—"

"You what?" He stared in shock. Then he set her on the seat, stood up, and roared, "Are you daft in the head?"

"You promised you would not get upset with me," she whined.

"That was before I kenned who you were hiding. Do you have any notion of the danger?" He bellowed. He paced the floor and roared to the ceiling.

"Dalziel! Do you want me to tell you everything or not?" she snapped.

"You mean there's more?" he shouted.

She cringed. "A lot more, Husband, please sit down."

"No, I will continue to pace before I burn this house down. Go on."

"Elsa has a list, a very important list that she needs to be delivered to the King of Scotland."

Dalziel stopped and stared at her. "Aye."

"She wants to give it to you. She... *we* are trusting you to deliver it to King Macbeth."

Dalziel was struck mute for the longest moment, reeling at her request. This was the very outcome he and Arrowsmith were trying to achieve. All this time they had been scouring the blasted countryside searching for Elspeth, and his wife had her hidden away right under their noses.

It humbled Dalziel that she now trusted him completely. Then he shuddered at the horrors of what could have happened to Clarissa if Siward's men had found them first.

Dalziel knew time was of the essence and he needed to get Elspeth to safety immediately.

"Where is Elspeth right now?" he asked.

"At the docks with Jean-Luc and Pierre," she replied.

"What the devil is she doing there?" he shouted.

"Stop yelling at me!" Clarissa shouted back. "Her family sent a missive via a French man at the dock. He will not pass it to anyone else but her."

"Stay here," Dalziel growled.

He went to his desk drawer and pulled out two daggers. Sheathed them to his belt.

"Why do you need those?" Clarissa asked, worried.

"In case I meet with trouble. Do you ken how many men are searching for Elsa right now? She should be out of sight, not at some dock acting like a bloody pirate!"

He bolted out the door and gave orders to Mr. Bell. Within minutes, a man brought his conveyance around.

Clarissa was already hot on his heels. "Dalziel! You are not leaving me behind. I will follow you if you do."

Dalziel paused; he knew she would make good on her threat. "Very well, get in you infuriating wench."

Chapter 13 - Decisions

The Docks, Bamburgh, Northumbria

The French captain was late, and Jean-Luc was getting worried. "Elsa, we need to go now. Tis dangerous to wait," he said in an urgent whisper.

"Just a few more minutes. The letter from France is important," Elsa pleaded.

Pierre, who was acting as their lookout, said, "There he is, by the third pier. He is signaling to you."

Elsa and Jean-Luc moved towards the shadowed figure. But when he stepped out into the light, it was not their contact but Lord Chamberlain. Two armed men appeared out of the mist to stand beside him.

"I knew you were still in *Bamburgh*, Lady Davenport. I just needed the right incentive to flush you out of hiding," Chamberlain said.

Elsa froze in fear as he leered at her. Jean-Luc pushed her behind him, shielding her as he held a knife. He knew the odds were not good, but he at least had Pierre somewhere in the mist as a backup.

"Do not risk yourself for me, Jean-Luc. You have a chance to escape," Elsa said and trembled as Chamberlain and his men stalked towards them.

"What of Jordie? You will leave him motherless to fend for himself?" Jean-Luc asked. He knew that was the incentive Elsa needed to abandon him. "When I give the signal, you run to Pierre, and you do not stop running," Jean-Luc whispered. He squeezed her hand. "Tell me you understand."

Elsa squeezed his hand in return.

Jean-Luc waited and just as Chamberlain was a couple of yards away, he turned to Elsa and said, "Now." He then charged straight at Chamberlain and his men as Elsa turned on her heel and ran.

Jean-Luc distracted the men and knocked Chamberlain off his feet. Chamberlain yelled, "Get her." His men tried to give chase, but Jean-Luc blocked their path. He took several blows to the head and face, but he continued to fight and slash out with his blade to give Elsa and Pierre a fighting chance. Jean-Luc thought he was going to die. He was wrong.

DALZIEL CROUCHED BESIDE an overturned boat harnessed atop the decking. He had removed his white leine in the carriage so he could easily blend into the dark. Bare-chested with a dagger in each hand, he had already figured out his plan of attack.

Pierre was crouched down beside him, cursing in French because Dalziel had physically tackled him and prevented him from running to Jean-Luc's aid.

"Bank your anger and learn some patience," Dalziel rebuked Pierre.

Pierre just glowered in return but remained in place.

Clarissa reluctantly watched from the safety of the carriage parked near a copse of Aspen trees. She wanted to help, but Dalziel was firm that if she disobeyed him, she could place them all at risk.

This was why Dalziel preferred to work alone. Civilians took up too much energy.

The moment Elsa started running, Dalziel said to Pierre, "Take the women to Stanhope. Dinnae deviate from the plan."

Pierre reluctantly nodded.

Dalziel sprinted down the dock towards the brawl, his eyes on the attackers who were about to murder Jean-Luc.

Jean-Luc had taken two blows to the face and was desperately trying to stop the men from running after Elsa. One had a knife, and his arm was poised, ready to stab Jean-Luc at his side. Jean-Luc was too busy focusing on the other men to notice.

Before the knife made contact, Dalziel appeared out of the mist and blocked the blade with one of his own. The sound of steel clashing against steel could be heard. The startled man had just registered what was happening when Dalziel plunged his other dagger into the man's neck. He staggered backward and fell into the water.

Dalziel then circled a second man as he twirled his blades with his wrists weighing up his opposition. The man charged at him. At the last minute, Dalziel dropped to his knees, crossed his arms, and slashed across the man's belly just below his rib cage, then rolled out of the way.

Dalziel saw the shock register on his face as his insides spilled out. He slumped face-first onto the ground. Dalziel wiped his bloody blades on the man's clothes.

Jean-Luc realized he had a savior and was solely focused on fighting Chamberlain, who had him in a headlock.

"Let him go," Dalziel said in a threatening voice.

Chamberlain released Jean-Luc, who rolled away from him, trying to catch his breath. Chamberlain had both hands up in the air in surrender, whilst Dalziel remained behind him, out of view. One arm holding him in place while his other hand held a dagger at Chamberlain's throat.

"Whoever you are, tis not your fight," Chamberlain said, fear tinging his voice as he felt the cold steel resting across his neck.

Dalziel did not speak or say a word. He only added more pressure with the blade.

In a state of panic, Chamberlain said, "That woman has something of mine. If she gives it to me, there will be no trouble I only want—"

Before he finished his sentence, Dalziel hit him on the side of the head with the dagger handle, knocking him out cold.

"*Je vous remercie,*" Jean-Luc said with heartfelt gratitude. Dalziel nodded in acknowledgment, then said, "Let's go." The two of them sprinted towards the trees.

Dalziel's Study, Stanhope Estate

LATER THAT NIGHT, IN the privacy of Dalziel's study, Pierre, Jean-Luc, Elsa, and Clarissa gathered around a large table discussing plans to keep Elsa and Jordie safe. Jordie was fast asleep in a guest-chamber above stairs. They had retrieved him from the *safe house*. Clarissa had already set everyone up in various chambers and they had partaken of a light supper together, courtesy of Mrs. Armstrong, who fussed over everyone like a mother hen. Especially Jordie, whom she doted on. Jordie just had to smile, and Mrs. Armstrong plied him with more sweets.

Once the servants had gone to bed, the group moved to the Study to discuss plans. Dalziel eventually joined them after he had washed the blood from his body and quietly listened as the group spoke in French.

Pierre had come up with a solution stating that it was best for Clarissa to go with Elsa to France and stay there until things were safe to return.

Suddenly, Dalziel interrupted them and said, "*Je crains d'être en désaccord!*" – I'm afraid I must disagree.

They all stopped talking. Mouth ajar, Clarissa asked, "You understand French?"

"Aye, a little. I ken enough." Dalziel glared at Pierre, who went bright red. Pierre had called him a '*sac à merde*' several times at the dock, which Pierre now knew Dalziel understood as meaning '*bag of shit.*'

"What do you mean you disagree?" Clarissa asked.

"You will not be hie-ing off to France, you daft woman."

"But we have to do something," Jean-Luc replied.

"I already have a plan," he told the group. "Tomorrow you will pack your bags."

"Why? Where are you sending me?" Clarissa asked in a panicked voice.

"I'm not sending you anywhere. I'm *taking* you, Elsa, and Jordie with me."

"Where?" they said as one.

"To the Highlands."

"But I cannot abandon—"

"I will make the arrangements to ensure the *safe house* remains secure."

"That is a sound plan," Pierre said.

"I agree. Better they are closer to Macbeth than Siward," Jean-Luc replied.

Dalziel's mind was made up. The only people he trusted most in the world were his family, his clan. It was time he introduced Clarissa to the MacGregors.

In the Dead of Night

THAT NIGHT, WHEN EVERYONE settled in their chambers. Clarissa was packing for her trip. Dalziel was downstairs in his study, finalizing estate matters before they left for the Highlands. Whilst packing, Clarissa realized she needed some vellum from her solar. She made her way down the hall and noticed the candles were still lit. She stepped into the room just as a hand clamped over her mouth and powerful arms held her in a firm grip.

It was Lord Chamberlain. "I knew twas your husband at the docks tonight, your carriage gave it away. He killed my men and now I will kill everyone in this house. Now, where is Elsa?"

Clarissa struggled to get out of his hold, but it was useless. She tried to bite his hand, but his grip was too firm. The only move she had left was to throw her head back and hopefully break his nose.

She did just that. Chamberlain loosened his grip slightly, but before Clarissa could scream, he grabbed her by the throat, so no sound escaped her lips.

Clarissa kicked and punched, but to no avail. Then she managed a lucky hit across his forehead. It drew blood over his eyes.

"You will pay for that." Chamberlain continued to choke her and raised his arm to backhand her when she heard a thunderous roar from the doorway.

Clarissa watched in slow motion as a rotating dagger flew past her head and lodged in Chamberlain's forehead.

His eyes rounded like saucers as he fell backward onto the floor, dead. Then there was silence.

"Did he hurt you, love?" Dalziel asked as he pulled her into his arms.

He saw her split lip and wanted to kill Chamberlain again.

"You killed him," she said.

"He was hurting you."

"You cannot just go about throwing knives at people like that," she scolded.

"I just did."

She opened her mouth but hung on as he lifted her into his arms and carried her towards their chambers. The noise and commotion had roused the household. Dalziel placed Clarissa in their room, then went out with the men to secure the premises and make sure no other enemies lurked in the house.

"Mr. Bell, there is a dead man in the study. Please send a message to the shire-reeve. Mrs. Armstrong, please send up a warm drink my wife has suffered a shock, then everyone please go back to bed.

The household did his bidding, and once it settled again, Dalziel saw to his wife.

"Will they punish you for killing a nobleman?" Clarissa asked as they got ready for bed.

"No."

"How do you know? Tis a serious crime."

"All will be well. I found him attacking *my* wife in *my* house. The law is on my side. Trust me, Clarissa, I ken these things."

"All right, Husband. I just could not live without you if they took you away."

He kissed her temple. "I feel the same way, that is why I did what I did."

Clarissa stroked his face gently with her fingers and whispered, "I love you, always."

It was the first time Clarissa had told him she loved him, and Dalziel's heart exploded with the knowledge.

That night he made love to her with an urgency he had never encountered before. They had been too long without each other, and their reconciliation coupling was frenzied and full of fervor. Dalziel lost himself deep inside her welcoming heat over again, to reassure himself she was very much alive. Each time he came, he hoped his seed took root. He caressed her stomach as he took her and wanted more than anything to see it rounded with his bairn, to feel their love grow into a family, touched by beauty and grace.

Chapter 14—The MacGregors

MacGregor Keep, Glenorchy, Scotland

Clarissa shuffled closer to Dalziel as the Great Hall doors opened with the sound of boisterous laughing and talking. Jordie and Elsa stood beside her.

A curvaceous dark-haired woman with a warm smile casually walked in, holding a basket full of herbs and flowers. She was laughing with a taller mixed-race woman who had a bow and quiver of arrows strapped to her back and a curved sword at her side.

Two large men brought up the rear. One had bronzed coloring he carried a baby boy in his arms, the other wore animal fur. He carried a large battle axe. Four children flanked their sides. Two girls and two boys. One boy carried a miniature battle axe, the other a miniature sword. One girl carried a bunch of flowers while the other held a bow and arrow. Clarissa guessed the children's weapon of choice matched their parents.

When the children spied Dalziel, they squealed with delight and ran towards him.

Clarissa stood stunned as her husband's face crinkled into a gigantic smile. He crouched down to their height with arms wide open just as the two girls crashed into him, throwing their arms around him. "Uncle Dee!" they exclaimed. The two boys followed suit. They all started chatting at once, clamoring for Dalziel's attention. Telling him stories of their adventures.

Dalziel tried to keep up and was so attentive to each of them. Clarissa realized Dalziel was truly home. This was his family. He loved them, and they loved him.

Dalziel temporarily broke away from the children to introduce Elsa and Jordan, and then Clarissa. "This is my wife, Clarissa." Dalziel pulled her closer to his side. She noticed the entire group gave smirks and grins while Dalziel just rolled his eyes.

"So, you are the reason Dalziel has been so secretive lately. I am Amelia. Welcome to our home." The dark-haired woman put her basket on the floor and hugged Clarissa. "This is my husband and our chieftain, Beiste and my baby boy Dalziel," — the man carrying the baby came forward and gave her a hug— "this is our daughter Iona,"—Amelia motioned to the girl with the flowers—"and this is our son Colban." The boy with the sword stepped forward and greeted her, although he seemed wary.

The family moved on to greet Elsa and Jordie. Beiste welcomed Dalziel with a firm handshake and warm smile, saying, "Brother, welcome home." Dalziel grinned at Beiste and kissed baby Dalziel on the forehead.

The man with the battle-axe stepped forward and introduced himself as Brodie Fletcher. He was Beiste MacGregor's Head Guardsman. He introduced both his children to her. Izara was the little girl with the bow and arrows and his son Thorfinn carried a tiny battle-axe. His wife Zala introduced herself and gave Clarissa a welcoming hug. She was a bowyer.

When Brodie saw Dalziel, he pulled him in for a giant bear hug and jokingly said, "Everyone missed you, Brother. Except for me. So, when are you leaving?"

Dalziel burst out laughing.

Clarissa watched the interaction between them all and smiled. There was so much love and affection, it was beautiful to witness. There was easy banter and no animosity.

"Right, come now, Clarissa and Elsa. We'll show you to your chambers so you can rest before supper." Amelia linked arms with Clarissa while Zala ushered Elsa and Jordan ahead of her. The children followed and started asking Jordie questions all at once.

"Wheesht! Stop pestering the poor lad. All of you, go see Cook in the kitchen for custard tarts." Amelia sounded exasperated.

"Yay custard tarts," they cried in unison. The inquisition was abandoned. They happily ran off towards the kitchens and the children had somehow absconded with Jordie as well. Last Clarissa saw, the poor lad was being dragged away by Iona and Colban. The former telling him she knew where the cook hides the sweets, the latter asking Jordie if he can wield a sword.

At the mention of wielding swords, Elsa paled, but Zala assured her Jordie would be fine and there were guards on hand always watching the bairns. Elsa relaxed.

Meanwhile, Beiste, Brodie, Dalziel, and his namesake sat around in the Great Hall, catching up on clan and family matters. Dalziel explained the full situation of what was happening in Northumbria and the attacks on Macbeth's contacts.

He missed conversing with his brothers. Dalziel trusted Beiste and Brodie above all others. Although not related by blood, they were brothers in arms, and they would die to protect each other and the clan. It had always been that way since they fostered together as boys with the Murrays.

"How is married life treating you, Brother?" Beiste asked, changing the subject.

"Tis good. Although she is a handful," Dalziel admitted and told them about the docks and the *safe house*.

Beiste roared with laughter when Dalziel told them about her swearing French cousins.

Brodie chuckled. "Sounds like she will fit right in here. Judging by how taken Amelia and Zala are with her, we will need to be on our guard lest they talk her into one of their harebrained schemes."

"Aye, that's what I'm afraid of," Dalziel replied, and winced.

Family Supper

THAT NIGHT, CLAN MACGREGOR gathered for a celebratory supper in the Great Hall to welcome Dalziel and his new bride and their guests, Elsa and Jordie.

Clarissa met Jonet, Beiste's mother, and Morag, Zala's adoptive mother. They both fussed over her and made it clear they were still mad Dalziel did not invite them to the wedding. Clarissa tried to defend him, but it was futile. She met many members of the clan, and one thing was clear, they highly respected her husband. Clarissa had never experienced this informality before. The family was boisterous; they were loud, and everyone enjoyed each other's company. It was not like Northumbria at all. There was no pretension. Just open, honest conversation.

Dalziel remained close by, even when he talked to other people. He would rest his hand on her thigh or on the back of her chair. Sometimes one hand would rest on her nape, and he would caress her skin with his thumb as he chatted to those beside him. She noticed the clan members grinning each time they caught one of his gestures, and she blushed.

Partway through supper, the doors flew opened, admitting a truly remarkably stunning young woman flanked by two disgruntled guardsmen carrying large bags of garments. She wore trews and an overlong tunic with a fur skin surcoat. She had a dagger sheathed to her side and a bow and quiver of arrows flung over her shoulder. Her eyes were striking, whilst her hair was a dark brown.

She took one look at Dalziel, dropped her belongings against the wall, and came running towards the table. He stood just in time to catch her as she hugged him and said, "Brother! You're home."

"Aye, lass, and by all appearances, you've been giving Kieran and Lachlan a headache." He raised an eyebrow.

"Nothing they didna deserve. I made them come garment shopping with me in the village and I made them stop at *every* market stall." She giggled.

Clarissa kept smiling, trying to work out who she was when Amelia said, "That's Beiste's sister, Sorcha. By the looks of things, she has dyed her hair. Tis usually golden like the sun."

Sorcha turned towards Clarissa and gave her an enormous smile. "You must be Dalziel's long-suffering wife, you poor woman." She bent down to peck a kiss on her cheek. "Tis good to meet you, Sister. Welcome." Then Sorcha was moving around the table to find a seat. She plonked herself beside Jordie and the children, declared she was famished, and dug into her food with gusto whilst the little ones clamored for her attention. Jordie kept staring at Sorcha like she was a faerie princess.

The rest of the evening passed by pleasantly except for when Morag said something to Elsa, which made no sense to anyone else, but it made Elsa blush. Clarissa made a mental note to ask her about it later.

That night, exhausted from their travels and a long day reuniting with family, Dalziel and Clarissa slept like the dead. Neither one having any energy to do much else other than hold each other through the night. As Clarissa heard her husband's steady breathing while his arms surrounded her, she felt a deep contentment she had never experienced before.

Big Teeth

THE FOLLOWING MORNING, Clarissa was dozing in her bed. Dalziel had woken her early for a rigorous bout of lovemaking before he left to go with the men, and it exhausted her. She had just fallen back to sleep when she heard several children speaking in hushed whispers near her bed.

"Da says she's *Angles*,"

"She's too pretty to be *Angles*."

"What's *Angles*?"

"Uncle Rory says tis a place where they eat bairns."

"I dinnae think I like Angles."

"Uncle Kieran said the men are like snakes."

"I heard aunt Amelia tell Ma, Uncle Kieran has a rash."

"Do you think she eats bairns?"

"You need big teeth to eat, bairns."

"Let's check her teeth."

Clarissa felt little fingers touching her mouth. She opened her eyes and quickly sat up.

The children screamed in fright and ducked under the bed except for the eldest girl, Iona.

"Auntie Clarissa, are you dying?" Iona asked.

Soon the door burst open, admitting Zala. "Iona MacGregor, stop harassing your aunt with your sickness and death questions." She walked into the room and shook her head.

Amelia followed behind her. "Go on with you, down to the kitchens now, all of you." She ushered the children out.

"Aw, we just wanted to see if she had big teeth," Thorfinn whined.

"I'll show you big teeth when I bite your necks." Zala ran after the children, trying to bite them. They squealed and hightailed it out of the room.

Colban remained. He scowled at Clarissa and said, "I'm watching you."

Amelia flicked him behind the ear. "Colban MacGregor, for your rudeness to your aunt, you will clean out the stables today. Now get yourself down to breakfast." She scolded.

"Aw Ma, I didna mean to be rude," Colban whined, but stomped out the door and muttered, "Bloody horses."

"Dinnae curse, or I'll make it two days shoveling poo in the stables," Amelia yelled.

She heard a 'hmph' sound as the door partially closed.

"Tis sorry I am about my son. He's just like his da, always brooding about like an ogre," Amelia said.

Zala was about to say something then paused and shouted, "Izara Fletcher, I ken you're still listening at the door. Get downstairs or I'll tell your da about your little boyfriend."

She heard a gasp and then footsteps running away.

Clarissa had never experienced so much noise, chatter, and activity first thing in the morning. But she had to admit it was nice. It felt like family.

Amelia sat on the bed. "So, you're the reason Dalziel was walking around with a spring in his step this morn?" She winked. "Good for you."

"Aye, no wonder he bolted to Northumbria during May Day celebrations. He must have been eager to bed his bonnie wife." Zala grinned.

Before Clarissa could respond, either way, both women moved about the room, getting her water ready and chatting as if they had known her their entire lives.

Soon, they were joined by Sorcha, who greeted her with a 'good morning' and slumped in the chair by the fire. Clarissa realized she would not get much privacy in the mornings.

"You ken Dalziel is very secretive. He did not even tell us he was married for several months," Amelia said. "When we found out, I was right sore about it. I wanted to box his ears in."

"Aye, Brodie was furious we were not invited and Jonet and Ma complained for months," Zala said as she gathered some drying cloths.

"I was very disappointed he did not even tell me." Sorcha pouted. "I would have made a wonderful bridesmaid, but that lout robbed me of the privilege."

"Ye've married a good man, Clarissa, but you need to make sure he doesna walk all over you," Sorcha said.

"Our men can be very... overprotective, and you've got to learn to fight for your right to do as you please," Zala said.

"Aye, and when you're angry dinnae let him sweet talk you with his charm because before you ken it, you'll be with child, and you'll forget what you were angry about." Amelia scowled and Zala burst out laughing.

"Tis not funny, Sister. I swear Beiste does not play fair."

"Aye, neither does Brodie. No matter how mad he makes me, he just has to gaze at me in a certain way and I want to climb him like a tree."

"Dalziel must be the same, I'm sure of it." Amelia winked at Clarissa.

"La la la la..." Sorcha started chanting loudly, covering her ears.

"Sorry Sister, we will not talk about your brothers anymore." Amelia smirked as Sorcha glowered at them.

"Well, we have bothered you long enough. When you're ready, come down to break your fast. The men will be back in time for supper," Zala said, and all three women left the room.

Clarissa got up, washed, and readied herself, then went downstairs to face the new day with her new family.

When she arrived at the dining table, she noticed Elsa and Jordie were already downstairs eating with the others and Jordie was in his element, laughing with the children while stuffing his face with honeyed toast. Elsa was a little more reserved, but she seemed well-rested, and she was enjoying the company. She sat beside Jonet, who was fussing over her.

Dalziel had told his family about Elsa and what she had endured at the hands of her husband. The MacGregors simply opened their arms and welcomed them. It did not matter that they were English; they accepted them because they loved Dalziel and he was family. Clarissa felt truly blessed to have married such a man who could garner that level of love and loyalty.

She wished that her brother Cedric was alive to be a part of this, and she missed him even more.

Safe Harbor

TWO DAYS LATER DALZIEL left for Macbeth's Castle in Dunsinane with several retainers.

He took the list and delivered it directly into Macbeth's hands. Macbeth activated his network, and they made contingency plans to ensure they protected his contacts. Macbeth also knew when Siward would attempt to dethrone him in favor of Malcolm III and Macbeth now knew the names and locations of Siward's spies in Scotland. His gratitude to Elspeth and Clarissa and Dalziel was immense.

Four weeks later, Dalziel received separate missives from Jean-Luc and Arrowsmith in Bamburgh that all was safe to return home. Elsa and Clarissa were no longer in danger.

Turns out they were wrong.

Chapter 15—She-Wolf

The Best Villains

It is often said that the best villains hide in plain sight. *She-wolf* was no exception. She had been hiding in plain sight from the very beginning because men were arrogant creatures. They assumed murderers could never be female, and strategy and cunning were the purviews of the male species. A faulty assumption that often led to their untimely deaths.

From France to Scotland to *Anglia*, she wove an intricate tapestry of lies and deceit all out in the open. She graced the beds of key men and gathered more information between the sheets than out of it. It never ceased to amaze her how many secrets men could divulge whilst in the throes of passion. Or even how much access they gave her to their homes as they slept. Never perceiving her to be a threat.

This ultimate flaw in male reasoning and arrogance was how she kept one step ahead of the lauded *Wolf*. She remained loyal to Earl Siward of Northumbria, her lover and a man who would raise her status when they unseated the Scottish king. When Malcolm III of Cranmore became king, Siward would share in Malcolm's glory and, by association, she would partake in his.

She sat quietly sipping her tea and staring out the window of her lavish bedchamber, waiting for her latest conquest to return. Her mind meticulously planning the next move. She smiled to herself because the best was yet to come. This time, she would strike at the heart of *the Wolf*!

The Betrayal

IT HAD BEEN A WEEK since Clarissa, Elsa and Jordie had returned to Northumbria.

Life resumed at a simpler pace now that they had eliminated the threat posed by the list.

With Davenport and Chamberlain dead, Lancet had closed down the *'Three Lords'* club and moved to Ireland.

Elsa was awaiting the next ship to France, which was due to leave in a few days, and Jean-Luc was to accompany her to ensure she and Jordie settled in.

Dalziel and Arrowsmith remained vigilant against the threat of the mysterious *She-wolf,* but both men were certain whoever it was, their avenue to wreak havoc had been severely limited.

As a result, Clarissa and Dalziel fell into a comfortable companionship, making plans for their lives and building a solid foundation for their marriage.

Clarissa suspected Dalziel took part in highly secretive work for Macbeth, and though she worried about his safety, she never pried into his affairs. She let him know should he ever need to share; he could trust she had the fortitude to bear it.

Dalziel loved that about her, knowing that she was his haven, and solace was enough. But by the same token, he would die to protect her from the heavyweight of the secrets he carried.

Therefore, when the betrayal happened, he was unprepared for the devastating effect it would have on him.

It was a sunny morning. Clarissa had gone with Martin to the *safe house* and Dalziel was working in his study when he was interrupted by Arrowsmith.

"What is this?" he asked when Arrowsmith handed him a rolled parchment.

"Tis a missive sent by your wife with her wax seal on it."

"Sent to whom?"

"The Earl of Northumbria. Twas intercepted by one of my men."

All else faded. Dalziel with shaking hands unrolled the parchment and, as he read, a visceral feeling of shock and disbelief merged into one. For there, before his eyes, was a missive to Earl Siward outlining every minute detail of his movements and his contacts.

The seal was his wife's; the writing resembled hers. Dalziel realized then he had been a fool and manipulated by the very woman he loved. The enemy lived under his roof.

"Who else has seen this?" he asked.

"Only me and my man. I dinnae want to act until we ken more details," Arrowsmith replied, concern in his voice.

"Aye, I appreciate it. Wait here."

Dalziel raced up to Clarissa's solar and began opening drawers, pulling out books on shelves, running his eye over everything, searching for further evidence. Finding nothing, he stormed to her bedchamber and pulled out clothes, undergarments, threw things on the floor.

Something caught his eye, a bundle of letters in the bottom drawer. He pulled them out. They were in French and English mentioning *'The White Bear.'* He knew then, with a sinking feeling in his heart, that he had been duped by the best. Her betrayal cut deep.

She had to die. But he could not, he would not do it. He drew the line at women and children. He still had doubts and he could not misstep with this. There had to be a logical explanation. His legs buckled and he dry, wretched, feeling like he was going to throw up. He swallowed down the panic as betrayal and doubt warred within. That is why he never got too close to women. Emotion clouded judgment. Feelings left one vulnerable. He had to think before he did anything rash.

The only recourse available to Dalziel was to send her away. It was the first time he failed to do his duty, and he knew then he could no longer be *The Wolf* for Macbeth. Not with his wife. For her own safety and his sanity, she needed to stay far away from him. He also needed to ensure no one else harmed her. He would remain calm and keep Arrowsmith on his side. Stall for the time until he figured out a way to protect Clarissa and save himself.

The Fall Out

CLARISSA RETURNED HOME in high spirits. Everything seemed to go well at the *safe house*. Since the list was no longer in their possession, they were all safer. Thanks to Dalziel, trusted guards now patrolled the *cove*.

She could not wait to tell Dalziel about her day. When she walked into the house, the mood was tense and somber.

Mr. Bell gave her a warning look. Mrs. Armstrong appeared on the verge of tears.

She frowned. "Whatever is the matter?" Clarissa asked.

"The Master needs to see you as a matter of import," Mr. Bell replied and led her to the study.

When she walked in, Dalziel stood by the fireplace, feet spaced apart, his hands linked behind his back, and he was glaring at her. She shuddered at the contempt he held in his eyes. Her blood ran cold. *Something was wrong.*

"What has happened, Husband?"

"You tell me, Miss Harcourt."

She flinched at his reference to her maiden name.

"I do not understand."

Dalziel moved away from the fireplace and walked to his desk. He picked up a bundle of parchments and threw the pile in front of her feet.

"Perhaps you could explain what those are?" he demanded.

She picked them up and said, "These are letters from Davenport's study. I told you that night I took them."

"No, you did not. You showed me one perfumed letter, but not those."

"It just slipped my mind. They've been there all this time. I have nothing to hide." She was confused at the implication.

"How convenient." Dalziel snorted. He picked up something else and threw it at her feet.

Clarissa was becoming increasingly angry with his rudeness.

"Cease throwing things at me and explain what you are accusing me of?" She huffed and picked up the wax seal. "Where did you get this? I have been searching for it everywhere?"

"Right," he said in disbelief. "It has been sitting on your desk."

"Dalziel, you better tell me why you are angry and why you are behaving this way."

"Miss Harcourt. What about this?" He threw a rolled parchment at her, which she caught before it landed on the floor.

She read it and paled. It bore her wax seal, but it was not her handwriting, yet the implication was that she was the writer, and the recipient was Siward.

"What is the meaning of this? I did not write this."

"Liar!" Dalziel yelled, and it was like he slapped her.

"You honestly do not believe I would be involved in something like this, do you?" Clarissa walked towards him and pleaded.

"I dinnae ken you at all." He stared at her with a coldness that seeped into her bones.

"You do not mean that, Husband, please think about it."

"Ye lied to me. I protected you, trusted you," Dalziel growled as he paced.

"Please, Husband, I need you to trust me. I do not understand—"

"Are you a contact for Siward?" He gripped her arms and shook her. "Tell me!" he roared.

"No, I am not. You need to listen to me. I did not write that letter."

"Convenient, that your wax seal is all over it."

"I lost it weeks ago. I've been hunting for it. You can ask Mrs. Arm—"

"Every word that falls from your lips is a lie."

Clarissa reached out for his arm and begged him. "Dalziel, tis me, your wife. I did not do this. Husband, what happened to the feelings—"

He recoiled from her touch. "Get out."

"What do you mean?" she gasped.

He shook his hand out of her grasp. "Dinnae ever touch me again, madam. You have the day to pack your things and remove yourself from my house."

He started walking towards the door. Clarissa ran after him, begging, "No, listen to me. I do not know how this happened. I swear I would not betray you. My seal has been missing and—"

Dalziel stopped at the door. He turned his head slightly, his back still to her, and said the words that would crush her heart forever. "Fair-warning, Wife, if our paths cross again, I will kill you myself." His voice was ice cold and devoid of all emotion.

With those parting words, he left and slammed the door behind him.

Clarissa collapsed and wept. Several minutes later, she gathered the remnants of her broken heart and her dignity and raised her chin. This was the last time she let her husband jump to conclusions, and this was the last time she trusted him with her heart.

Clarissa ran to her chambers and noticed the unruly state of her room. She gathered only the things she brought with her, enough to fit into a tiny bag, everything else she left behind.

She was grateful at least she still had the cottage, and Martin and Ruth. They would not starve. She still had card games and they could take up smuggling to fall back on to keep afloat. Clarissa was resourceful. She still had her family, and France. *She would survive.*

Mrs. Armstrong and the entire staff were forlorn. "Mistress, he will calm down. Dinnae be hasty. He will be back. I ken the master loves you."

Clarissa stared at her with tears in her eyes. "Not enough, Mrs. Armstrong. Not enough. He would not even listen to me."—She shook her head as the tears streamed down — "Thank you for your kindness." — She looked around at the staff — "I will never forget you. If you ever need help, you only need to ask." Clarissa choked out the last words. Then turned and moved towards the main door.

"Mistress, please reconsider. The master is a hothead, and he will change his mind," Mr. Bell said.

"Thank you, Cecil, but even if he does, nothing will induce me to change mine," Clarissa replied with finality.

By the evening, she was back at Driftwood Cottage, and it broke her heart.

It poured down with rain that night. She snorted. *At least the roof is fixed.* She laughed at the absurdity of her predicament, then she burst into tears and wept bitterly.

That night in the empty cold bedchamber at Stanhope, Dalziel recoiled from his inner turmoil. *Bloody Sassenach!* He threw his scotch glass at the fireplace; it smashed into a million pieces. He felt the betrayal. And it hurt. It hurt like hell. A dull ache gripped his heart because he knew that his life would never be the same.

The Morning After

EARLY THE NEXT MORNING, Clarissa dragged herself out of bed. She needed to remain busy. Others relied on her, and no matter the inner turmoil gripping her now, the *safe house* came first. She went on as she had before. Striving to keep them all safe. She owed it to Cedric; she was resilient, and she could survive anything.

That same morning, Dalziel noticed Clarissa only took the things she had arrived with. She had left everything else behind.

"Why did she not take the money?" he asked his clerk.

Rupert replied, "She wanted nothing to remind her of you."

He flinched. "How the hell is she supposed to live without funds?" Dalziel asked, feeling concerned. Women without money often found themselves in compromising positions.

Rupert just shrugged.

"I want you to send funds to the *safe house*. At least I ken she willna reject money for the women and bairns."

❦

ANOTHER THREE LONG days and two even longer nights passed by. Dalziel's staff were not talking to him. Mrs. Armstrong stopped making him scones. Mr. Bell gave him a curt reply whenever he asked about anything. And every minute he battled with the need to go to Clarissa on the one hand and the need to remain angry with her betrayal. When he thought he would soften, he remembered she had betrayed him, just like his mother had betrayed his da. He had promised himself he would never fall in love with an English woman, and he had gone and done the very thing.

❦

Broken

CLARISSA CRIED INTERMITTENTLY during certain periods of the day. Her soul felt broken. Dalziel discarded her like unwanted garbage. That hurt the most. She missed Cedric more than ever. He always knew what to do, and he always cheered her up when things were bleak. Without him, she just felt an ache soul deep inside, and she knew her body and mind were going through a grieving process again.

She was so grateful for her family. Pierre and Jean-Luc raged and cursed Dalziel, and it was all Clarissa could do to stop Pierre from calling him out with swords. She did not have the heart to tell Pierre he would lose.

Martin and Ruth were her shelter from the storm. They kept her sane and the women and children at the *safe house* kept her busy. Martin expressed several times that if he saw Dalziel again, he would kill him. As far as her family was concerned, his name was never to be mentioned again. Clarissa was happy with that mandate. She knew that time would heal her wounds and someday Dalziel would be nothing but a distant memory. She resolved to keep nothing around her that would remind her of him.

Four days later, her morning sickness began.

***

CLARISSA SAT IN HER garden at the Cottage and just stared out at the sea. It soothed her troubled soul to watch the magnificent ocean do its thing.

"Will ye tell him about the bairn?" Ruth asked her.

"Tell him what? That the woman he despises carries his babe? No, I will not tell him a thing."

"Do not be hasty. Just think about it," Ruth said.

Clarissa replied, "No, he made it clear he wanted nothing to do with me. He thinks the worst of me."

Ruth came and sat down beside her. "Think of the babe, Mistress. Do not let pride get in the way."

"I am thinking of the babe, Ruth. I will not raise a child in a loveless marriage with a father who despises their mother. That was my childhood. I will not repeat it. Besides, once the annulment comes through, it will be over. I do not want him to stay married to me because of a child."

"Do you have any notion who would write that letter pretending it was you?" Ruth asked.

"None. And I no longer care."

Arrowsmith

ARROWSMITH WOKE IN a haze. Although he knew it was a late night, he had no recollection of why he felt sleepy. Arrowsmith could just see daylight peeking in through the windows and he knew he was in his bedchamber. He rubbed his face but was prevented from rising because of a long, slender leg lying atop his own. The nude body of a woman was beside him when he turned his head. He gently pushed her away and rolled out of bed. He was naked, his head felt fuzzy, and he reached for his robe and quickly wore it.

He could not recall how on earth he had ended up in bed with *this* woman? He had broken off all ties since her last visit and had not taken up with anyone else since. He rubbed his forehead. This was not good. The mind fog refused to clear Arrowsmith felt as if he was going to throw up.

"Mmm, while I admire the front of you immensely, the back of you is just as striking," she purred.

Arrowsmith swung around and asked, "What happened last night?" He stared at her as she lay on her side, partially covered by the bedsheets, her breast spilling over the side exposed.

"Why darling, are you not happy to see me?" She got up, dropped the sheet, and shuffled on her knees towards him. "You were thrilled to see me last night; in fact, I am a little sore from your eager welcome."

He scanned the room. There were no sponges or vials of vinegar, no telltale signs they had coupled. His wine was still intact. He had not imbibed. He had gone to bed with a headache, and that was all.

She took his hand and placed it on her breast. "Mayhap you could come back to bed?" She pouted.

Arrowsmith pulled away and said, "Please leave."

There was a knock at the door, and Barret, his valet, entered. "Miss, why are you still here? I insist you stop playing this charade."

Arrowsmith was confused. "What charade?"

"You had a sleeping draught last night for your headache. Your lady friend here arrived this morn insisted on seeing you. I turned her away, but she somehow got into your chambers when my back was turned." He gave Arrowsmith a knowing look.

Arrowsmith turned back to her.

"We did not couple at all, did we?"

"Not if you managed it while dead to the world," Barret replied.

Arrowsmith gritted his teeth. "I have told you tis over and you need to leave."

She just shrugged her shoulders, donned her clothing, and meandered out the door.

"Make sure she leaves," Arrowsmith told Barret.

Arrowsmith poured cold water on his face. Relieved he had not coupled with her. She was becoming persistent. He saw to his needs and took a bath. He was dressing when a thought occurred to him.

He walked over to his bedside table and opened the drawer. "Damn!" His notes were missing. Then the realization set in.

Thirty minutes later, Arrowsmith bounded up the stairs to his ex-lover's abode, and no servants were in attendance. He barged through the Town House, calling her name with no answer. The place seemed empty, as if she were halfway packed to move.

Arrowsmith raced up the stairs and began searching her rooms. But it was when he rummaged through her things something caught his eye. A box of pins. But not just any pins. They were the same color pins used to fasten the French notes to the dead bodies. His blood ran cold.

He started rummaging through other drawers and found parchments and papers a woman like her should not have access to.

Then he knew he had to see Dalziel. A grave injustice had been committed and now they needed to find *She-wolf* before she took Arrowsmith's latest secrets and wreaked havoc.

Sleeping with the Enemy

AFTER THE LONGEST WEEK of his life, Dalziel had calmed down enough to see reason. There was no way Clarissa could have sent that letter, surely not. Things made little sense. Mrs. Armstrong had corroborated Clarissa's version that she had lost the wax seal several weeks ago and she added that around the same time Clarissa also lost her gold chain and they had all helped her search, to no avail.

Dalziel needed to see his wife. He was working out a way to beg and grovel for her forgiveness when Arrowsmith arrived unannounced. He sported a troubled look.

"What is it?"

Arrowsmith started pacing. "I thought about that parchment that your wife supposedly sent. I ken in the past I have accused her of things, but instinct told me I was missing something."

"What was it?"

Arrowsmith felt embarrassed, then spilled it all.

"Your wife is not the only woman who kens things about our movements."

"Who are you talking about?"

"The woman I had been... sleeping with. The one who was there when you came to visit."

"Aye, what about her?"

"Sometimes I shared things with her when we were... together, and I felt the need to share some of my burdens."

Dalziel gritted his teeth. "Tis very dangerous to share anything with a woman you barely ken."

"Aye, but there are times she asks questions, and before I ken it, my tongue just loosens."

"Why?"

"Because she is vapid and vacuous like she fathoms nothing deeply, so I found it easy to unburden, thinking she would have no notion of what I speak."

"So, you thought her a dunce and, therefore, safer with secrets?"

Arrowsmith nodded.

"What has caused you to suspect her?"

"I found these in her Town House." He pulled out a box of pins.

Dalziel stared and made the connection. "Those are Lenora's pins. She used to use them for play."

"Do you ken something else familiar about them?" Arrowsmith asked.

Dalziel inspected it closer and cursed, "Fuck! They are the same pins used for the notes."

"Aye."

"Wait, I'm confused. Lenora was your lover?"

"No, her sister was my lover, only I did not ken their secret relationship until today, when I went through her things."

"Who is her sister?" Dalziel asked.

"Harmony Durham and I believe she is Earl Siward's mistress." Arrowsmith grimaced.

"Bloody hell, Arrowsmith, do you ken what this means?" Dalziel was pacing now.

"Aye, I have been feeding information directly to Siward, and all this time, I was warning you not to do the very thing I have just done." Arrowsmith was furious with himself.

Dalziel was grim. "This explains why Cedric Harcourt was killed. He was courting Harmony as well."

"Damn!" Arrowsmith cursed.

"Aye, she has played us all for fools. She wormed her way into Cedric's affections and no doubt found out he was a contact for Macbeth. Then she found her way into your bed and did the same," Dalziel said.

Arrowsmith was livid more so with himself. "I should have kenned she was too keen on me for a reason. The amount of times I would find her in my home unannounced. She had ample time to find things and hear things. Places, names."

"Aye, and she could easily have stolen the wax seal. She is close to Clarissa and has visited here occasionally."

Arrowsmith said, "She also kens about the *safe house*. She could have even tipped off Goldie that day and she kenned we were keeping a vigil of the 'Three Lords' club."

"Where is she now?" Dalziel asked.

"I dinnae ken I could not find her, but she is dangerous, Dalziel."

Dalziel was gripped by a sense of urgency to see Clarissa. He said, "Arrowsmith, I need to see my wife. She may be in danger." Both men were already moving out the door.

Frenemies

CLARISSA WAS WORKING at the *cove,* going through accounts. The house was mostly empty as the occupants were down at the beach.

The guards Dalziel continued to hire around the property had gone down to the beach to keep watch over the women and children.

She heard someone banging on the door. When she peered outside, it was Harmony on the doorstep.

Clarissa unlocked the door. "Harmony, is everything all right?"

Harmony pushed the door wide open and stepped over the threshold. "Where's Elsa?" she demanded in a stern voice.

Everything about her countenance was different. Gone was the ditsy pouting woman they all knew, and in her place was someone entirely different. Clarissa stared at a point behind Harmony and saw men coming up the footpath. Acting on instinct, Clarissa shoved Harmony backward out the front door and pushed it closed, locking it. Harmony tumbled backward into two men trying to get in the door.

Clarissa then turned on her heel and ran towards the back of the house, shouting a warning. She was just about out the back door when a large man stepped out in front of her. It was Lord Lancet.

"Where is Elspeth?" he demanded.

"She is not here."

"Do not lie to me!" he yelled.

"I swear to you, she is not here. She left weeks ago."

Lancet stared at her a moment, then said, "Liar."

Clarissa heard a scream and turned to see another man pulling Elsa out of one room. She was kicking, scratching, and punching to break his hold, but it was futile. Clarissa had never seen Elsa fight so hard. She tried to assist, but Lancet grabbed her from behind.

It was then Harmony meandered towards Clarissa. "You should have been nicer to me, Ris. I might have let you live."

"Why are you doing this?" Clarissa asked, not recognizing this version of Harmony at all.

"Because I am part of a *cause* as well and the only thing standing between me and victory is Elsa here and you."

"Tis why you both have to die," Lancet said.

"We have nothing to do with this," Clarissa implored.

"That's where you're wrong. Elsa here knows too much about Lancet's dealings," Harmony replied. Then she turned to Clarissa. "You, on the other hand, are completely innocent, but unfortunately I need you dead as well."

"Why?"

"Because you are the heart of *The Wolf* and to destroy him, I need to cut out his heart."

Clarissa panicked when Harmony pulled out a long knife. "I do not even know *the Wolf*," she said. "This is madness."

Clarissa's mind was reeling. She was going to die along with her unborn babe all because of this *Wolf* person and the crazed lunatic wielding a knife. She wanted to weep and laugh in equal measure.

"Oh, but you do know *the Wolf*," Harmony replied with a wicked grin. "You are married to him."

Clarissa stilled. She remembered Dalziel mentioned an assassin for the King of Scotland. But at the time he made it seem as if the assassin was merely an acquaintance. All the pieces came together when she realized Dalziel, her husband, was *the Wolf*. Clarissa just hoped she lived long enough to kick him in the balls for lying to her.

Chapter 16 - The Wolf

Dalziel reached the *safe house* and sensed something was wrong. He went to run into the house, but Arrowsmith stopped him. "Calm down. There's five of them inside, another one keeping watch from the side entrance."

They made a quick plan of attack, then parted ways. Dalziel ran along the other side of the building and climbed. There was no place he could not enter. This was what he did best, this was who he was. No one crossed *the Wolf* and survived.

Dalziel was high on the structure and leaned into the windows. He slipped in through the side window of the second floor, then kept his steps light as he made his way to the landing for a better view below.

He unsheathed his blades and made his way down the back staircase. He could hear the conversation below and saw one man standing watch at the bottom of the stairs.

The kill was quick and silent. Dalziel caught his lifeless body and quietly lowered it onto the floor. He stepped over him and made his way closer to the front entrance, where they had stationed another man in the hall. He was startled when Dalziel appeared before him. His throat was cut before he could scream. Dalziel dragged his body out of view.

He then crouched to get a better view into the front room, and that was when he saw a man holding Elsa in a tight grip. He was standing beside an open window. Dalziel also saw Clarissa being held by Lancet.

But it was the view of Harmony pacing between them, wielding a large knife that had his blood running cold. Dalziel crawled along the floor, hiding behind furniture until he was closer.

He could incapacitate one person, but not all three, without risking injury to either Clarissa or Elsa. He was weighing up his options when the answer to his dilemma came by Arrowsmith and a flying arrow through the window. It lodged in the back of Elsa's attacker, who shouted in pain and released her, then stumbled away from the window.

That was all the time Dalziel needed to finish the job. And he did, with precision. He hurled a dagger at Lancet's neck. His aim struck true, and Lancet let go of Clarissa and crumpled to the floor.

He threw his second dagger at Harmony's weapon. It knocked the knife out of her hand, and it clattered to the floor. Dalziel then charged and threw the force of his body at her, knocking her off her feet and rendering her momentarily unconscious. Clarissa ran forward and kicked the knife out of Harmony's reach.

Arrowsmith now entered the building and incapacitated Elsa's attacker whilst a relieved Dalziel caught Clarissa as she ran into his arms and burst into tears.

"Shh... love, tis all right. You're safe now," he kept whispering to calm her. The couple lost in their own world.

Elsa had recovered from her fright and was about to fetch Jordan from his hiding place. She faltered when she saw Arrowsmith up close. He had the same reaction.

"Beth?" Arrowsmith said in shock as he stared at Elsa.

"Ewan?" she whispered and paled, as if she had just seen a ghost. "They said you were dead."

"You left without a word," Arrowsmith said at the same time.

Their shock was interrupted by the cry, "Mama!" as a bundle of dark brown hair flew into Elsa's arms. "Mama. I did what you said, and I hid."

"Good boy, Son." She stroked his hair.

Arrowsmith stared at the back of the little boy, and then he glanced up at Elsa. His eyes shuttered, replaced with a scalding expression. He was about to walk away when Jordie turned to face him.

"Thank you for saving my mama," Jordie said.

Arrowsmith glanced down at Jordie to respond, then stilled because staring up at him was a replica of his own hazel eyes. It knocked the breath from his lungs.

His eyes whipped back to Elsa, his brow furrowed, seeking affirmation if Jordie was his. She blushed and averted her eyes. The world tilted on its axis and Arrowsmith felt as if someone had punched him in the gut with a boulder. He gritted his teeth and clenched his fists.

"Tis my pleasure, Son. Your ma and I go a long way back. Isn't that right, Beth?"

Elsa nodded, all the while Arrowsmith kept his gaze steadily on her.

Jordie asked, "Mama, can I have something to eat now?"

"Of course. Let me get you away from here." She gave a weak smile.

"Will you join us, mister?" Jordie asked Arrowsmith.

Elsa seemed embarrassed. "Jordie, I do not think he has time to eat right now."

Arrowsmith glared at her. "On the contrary, I would love to join you and your ma."

He took Jordie's hand in his, and led them to the kitchen, being careful to shield Jordie from the dead bodies. Elsa had no choice but to follow beside him.

As Jordie chatted away, Arrowsmith muttered, "You gave him my middle name?"

"Aye." Elsa inhaled a sharp breath.

Arrowsmith kept his eyes straight ahead as they walked. Then he reached out and grabbed her hand, clasping it in his own as he pulled her closer. "Seems we have much to discuss, Beth."

Elsa exhaled as if she had been holding her breath for seven years and for the first time in a long time, she could breathe again.

Revenge

WHEN HARMONY CAME TO, she was tied to a chair in the office of the *safe house*. Arrowsmith and Dalziel stood with their arms folded, ready to interrogate her, and Clarissa hovered in the background. They all wanted answers.

Earlier, with the help of the guards, the dead bodies were removed, and the house was put back in order. They directed the women and children to the other end of the house so they could have time alone with Harmony.

Harmony chuckled, "Gentleman to what do I owe this pleasure?" She mocked.

"Why did you kill Lenora?" Dalziel asked. It had puzzled him to no end.

"Because I was tired of the stupid sow. She had one task to accomplish, and she failed repeatedly."

Dalziel realized then Lenora was also in on the scheme. "And what was that role?" he asked.

"To get close to you and extract your secrets, but she was useless." Harmony spat out. "I gave her one last chance. All she had to do was steal some things from your wife and she could not even do that without getting herself thrown out of your house."

"But she's your sister," Arrowsmith said.

"That's why she disappointed me the most. She was weak. I had no use for her."

"You killed Cedric," Clarissa said, interrupting them all.

"Yes, twas rather simple. He never saw it coming. Besotted fool."

"But why? He would never harm a soul." Clarissa needed to understand.

"Because Siward demanded it. Cedric was passing secrets to Macbeth. I only had to get close and make sure I reported his movements, but he became suspicious, so he left me no choice."

"How can you do this with no remorse?" Clarissa asked.

"Easily Ris. Cedric thought me a dunce, so I played along. Oh, the shock on his face when he realized I was smarter than he was. Twas priceless. Same as all the other contacts I killed who thought me stupid. Even you fell for it." Harmony smirked at Arrowsmith.

Something snapped inside Clarissa when she thought of her poor brother, Cedric.

"I want to beat you to death right now, but I will not hit a woman," Arrowsmith replied.

"I will, and I will kill you!" Clarissa screamed as she stormed past him, fists clenched. She drew her arm back and her fist connected with Harmony's nose. It broke, and Harmony screamed as her head lurched backward. Clarissa then straddled her and started slapping her and pulling her hair. Harmony kept screaming.

Dalziel grabbed Clarissa around the waist and lifted her away to prevent her from doing damage to herself. Clarissa fought like a wildcat, trying to get loose. She pointed at Harmony and yelled, "You are dead! You are dead!"

Arrowsmith was stunned at Clarissa's behavior and tried to stifle a laugh.

"Stop laughing or I'll punch you too," Clarissa shouted at Arrowsmith.

Arrowsmith backed away just in time, narrowly missing a fist to the face and a kick to the groin.

"Ris! Calm down, tis over. Harmony will get what she deserves. Men are coming to take her to Macbeth. She will never see the light of day again."

That seemed to appease Clarissa, and she calmed down. Dalziel carried her into the next room and sat down with her in his lap. He soothed her as she mourned the loss of Cedric all over again.

Regret

THREE DAYS HAD PASSED since the attack on the *safe house* and Dalziel was still no closer to reconciling with his wife. After the initial shock and anguish of the day, Clarissa refused to return to Stanhope Estate. Although grateful Dalziel had come to her rescue, being in his arms again felt too good and, should he change his mind again in the future, she would be bereft. Instead, she remained at the cottage and awaited an annulment.

Dalziel was in the sitting room of Driftwood Cottage, pleading once again for her to forgive him and return home. "Please forgive me, Love. I dinnae ken what else I can do to prove to you I will never mistrust you again. I need you to come home."

"I am home." Clarissa stared out the window.

"I love you, Ris."

"I believe you said that once before." She sighed and closed her eyes. She felt nothing. Numb.

"I will continue to care for you, no matter what happens," Dalziel replied.

"You are *the Wolf*?" Clarissa surprised him with her question.

"Aye, I am. I am deeply sorry this happened because of me."

"Tis all right, Dalziel, truly. I understand there are secrets one must keep protecting others."

Dalziel sighed with relief, then tensed at her next words.

"If you wish to care for me, please grant me an annulment. I think tis best we go our separate ways.

Dalziel felt shattered. "Ris, please forgive me. Please let me make it up to you." His voice was guttural, beseeching.

She turned and their eyes locked for the first time. She saw the sincerity and love there, but she could not risk her heart again. He had almost destroyed her. "Believe me when I say I have forgiven you. I just cannot go back to how things were." She turned and walked towards the back room before saying, "Martin, please escort Lord Stanhope out."

"Ris please." Dalziel moved to stop her.

Martin blocked his way. "Not now me lord, give her more time, Son."

Dalziel left. His heart was heavy and his soul empty. The light had gone, leaving a dark shadow of regret.

Chapter 17 – The Intervention

The Great Hall, MacGregor Keep, Glenorchy

"'Tis true, I was a damned fool. I had a bonnie wife and now she doesna love me anymore. What would you do if you were me?" Dalziel asked his ten-month-old namesake.

The latter responded with a loud fart and then burped up milk all over Dalziel's shoulder.

Dalziel grimaced. "I dinnae think farting and burping tis the answer, Son."

"He is just like his da, here let me take him." Amelia chuckled as she took her baby son from Dalziel and gave him a cloth to wipe his shirt.

"Where are the others?" Dalziel asked as he cleaned the baby vomit.

"They're down by the loch. The bairns were getting underfoot, so Beiste and Brodie took them swimming.

"And where's Zala? Sorcha? Jonet?"

"Zala is resting. Poor thing is expecting twins again. Can you believe it? Brodie's seed must be potent because he keeps planting two bairns at a time."

"Well, the way they go at each other, they'll probably have a dozen the next time I see them." Dalziel snorted.

"Wheesht. If Zala hears you, she'll likely stab you for even saying it out loud."

Dalziel watched Amelia fuss over her son. He had visions of Clarissa as a mother to their bairns, which made him miss her even more.

Dalziel arrived at MacGregor Keep unannounced. He just needed to be around his family. Even if it was just for a few days. He already told Amelia what had happened between him and Clarissa, and she had lent a sympathetic ear to his woes. Dalziel asked Amelia *not* to tell Beiste and Brodie yet until he had time to explain.

"Sorcha and Jonet have gone to the village with a few retainers. Apparently,"—Amelia lowered her voice to a whisper — "dinnae say anything to anyone yet, but I think Sorcha has caught the eye of a young man in the village."

"What young man? What does he do for a living? Who is his family?" Dalziel growled.

Amelia just rolled her eyes. The men were so protective of Sorcha, the poor girl could barely breathe.

Before Amelia could explain, the door to the Great Hall opened and in strolled Brodie and Beiste, with a large brood of loud, excited children trailing behind. They comprised their children, plus several children of other clansmen.

They saw Dalziel and immediately ran to greet him. He grinned and braced as they launched themselves at him, all talking at once about their swimming expedition, all competing for his attention, their voices growing even louder.

"All right, that's enough. Let your uncle have some breathing room. Iona, take everyone to the kitchen, Cook's got apple pie for you all," Beiste said as the children abandoned the adults and took off down the hall.

Beiste made his way to Amelia and kissed her on the cheek, then kissed the baby's head. He greeted Dalziel and sat down beside him.

Brodie joined them on the opposite side of the table and said, "Bairns are exhausting. I dinnae ken how I'm going to survive another two in a few months."

"Where's Clarissa?" Beiste asked.

Before he could ask anything else, Dalziel demanded, "What's this about Sorcha and some boy in the village?"

"What boy?" Beiste and Brodie yelled in unison.

"Dalziel, I told you not to tell!" Amelia scowled at him.

Beiste and Brodie turned to Amelia with dagger eyes and Beiste asked, "How long have you kenned this, Amie?"

"What's his name and where does he live because I will crush him," Brodie said and slammed his fist on the table.

Amelia had no ready come back so instead, she deflected and shouted, "Dalziel accused Clarissa of betraying him and turned her out of their house onto the street with only the clothes on her back. But she didna betray him, and now she has left him."

That had Brodie and Beiste whipping back to glare at Dalziel.

"You turned your wife out of your house with only the clothes on her back?" Beiste looked disgusted.

"You falsely accused that bonnie woman and abandoned her on a stinking, Northumbrian street?" Brodie was appalled.

"Are you daft, Brother? It doesn't matter how angry you are with your wife; you never throw her out like stale bread." Beiste shook his head in disappointment.

It was Dalziel's turn to glower at Amelia. "I asked you to wait until I had a chance to tell them!"

"Did you? Well, I best go check on the bairns," Amelia replied and hurried out of the hall with his namesake.

THAT NIGHT IN THE GREAT Hall, Dalziel felt even more depressed. He had imbibed far too much than he normally did, and that only lead to maudlin feelings.

Brodie, Beiste, and Dalziel sat around the fire in armchairs drinking mead when Zala appeared. She had recently heard about what Dalziel did to Clarissa, and she was not impressed.

"Brodie, please tell that man beside you that supper is ready."

"Tell him yourself, Zala. He's sitting right there."

She scowled at Brodie and stormed off without a word.

Dalziel rolled his eyes.

"The women are annoyed with you, Brother. They think you are a daft prick. Tis only what I heard from Ma," Beiste said.

"Aye, Morag called you bloody stupid. Just thought I'd throw that in as well, Brother," Sorcha said as she walked past.

"No matter how infuriating a woman is, ye dinnae kick her out. What message do you send to everyone else? Tis humiliating," Brodie said.

Beiste lowered his voice and said, "Do you ken the number of times I have wanted to kick Amelia out of the Keep, but didna do it?"

"Ha! I'd like to see you try, Beiste MacGregor!" Amelia shouted from the other side of the hall.

"I swear that woman has unnatural hearing," Beiste grumbled. Then yelled, "I love you, Amie." He chuckled when she snorted in response.

"She has a point Beiste, I doubt you'd get very far without being attacked by every member of the clan if you tried throwing Amelia out," Brodie replied.

"My point is, Amelia and I, we disagree all the time, Dalziel. There's a misunderstanding, mistakes are made. Angry words are exchanged. But I would never, ever tell her to leave. Women take those things seriously."

"Aye, if Clarissa left you, tis because you told her to, not because she wanted to," Brodie piped in.

Dalziel stared into his cup. "She begged me to listen to her, she begged me to trust her, and I let her down. She'll never take me back now."

"And so she shouldn't, you stupid man. I hope you suffer until your bawsack shrivels up like rotten grapes drying in the sun. Now eat something." Zala slammed some food on the small table in front of the men and stormed off again.

Brodie reached out and hauled her onto his lap. Zala shrieked in surprise, then settled when Brodie planted a smacking big kiss on her lips.

"What was that for Brodie Fletcher?" Zala asked.

"The sight of you getting all feisty while you have my bairns inside you makes me hard."

Zala burst into giggles when he tried to kiss her again. "Get off me, you randy bear." Brodie let her go, and she just shook her head and strode to the kitchen.

Dalziel was sick to death of happy couples cavorting around him while he was dying inside. Coming home was not exactly the best plan he had ever had. *Maybe he should go some place where the married couples were miserable and bickered all day.*

Brodie watched Dalziel brood. He felt for him. Brodie knew what it was like to be separated from one's wife, and he empathized. He only hoped Dalziel and Clarissa would come to their senses before it was too late.

A couple of days later, a call came from a neighboring clan requesting help to control a skirmish with raiders. Dalziel, feeling despondent, answered the call and threw himself into the fight with no thought of the consequences.

Driftwood Cottage, Bamburgh, Northumbria

"WHO IS IT, MARTIN?" Clarissa asked.

"Tis a Highlander here to see you."

Clarissa tensed, wondering who it was. The door opened and Brodie Fletcher filled her doorway.

"Brodie?" She smiled, happy to see him, but he had a dark expression. Enough to worry her. "Is everything all right?" she asked. She could feel panic rising, wondering if something had happened to Dalziel.

When Brodie spoke next, her greatest fear was realized.

"Sorry, Clarissa, I come on an urgent matter. Tis Dalziel."

"What about him?" Clarissa stood and dropped her sewing on the floor.

"Dalziel took a knife wound. He may not survive. Amelia has done all she can, but he has been calling for ye. Me and my men have come to fetch you."

"Then I must least at once. What on earth happened?" Clarissa felt sick with fear and started moving about."

"He tried to break up a skirmish and got outnumbered with raiders, tis heartbreaking."

"I told him to take better care of himself, that stupid, stubborn man!" she shouted, unshed tears gathering as she ran to her bedchamber to pack.

Ruth was by her side and helping her while Martin saw to Brodie and his retainers.

At that moment, Clarissa realized she had been a fool to not take Dalziel back. She loved him still. She never stopped loving him and she could not bear to lose him now. What a strange twist of fate, she thought. Now he would never know about the babe if he died before she reached him. She prayed she got there in time; she wanted to tell him so much that she loved him and always would.

The next few days, they set a hard pace to get to Dalziel. Time was of the essence, and Clarissa felt panicked the entire way. Her frustration grew when Brodie and his men kept trying to slow her down as they forced her to take rest breaks. He wanted her to take care of herself. Clarissa wanted to shout at Brodie that if Dalziel died before she arrived, she would beat him to death.

When they finally arrived at MacGregor Keep, Brodie had barely dismounted his horse when Clarissa had jumped down and was running for the Great Hall doors. Without waiting, she pushed them open and ran inside. She glanced around and started screaming, "Where is Dalziel? Where is my husband?"

She was beside herself with worry and getting agitated. No one was taking her to him. Her hair was disheveled, her face was smudged with dirt, and she had a crazed glint in her eye.

A startled serving woman just pointed towards a door down the hallway and stepped out of her way.

Clarissa ran and threw the doors open. It was filled with men sitting around a large table discussing matters, and there, slouched in a chair near the head of the table, was Dalziel. Healthy as can be and leaning back against the backrest.

He stood immediately and just stared at her. His expression one of shock and disbelief. Silence descended over the room as all eyes rested on her.

Clarissa realized then she had ridden in a panic all the way from Northumbria, thinking her beloved Dalziel was dead, fearing the worst, and meanwhile he was just sitting there. She could not believe what she was seeing.

"Ris love, what has happened?" Dalziel was striding towards her, concern and love shining in his eyes.

Brodie ran in behind her, a little out of breath. "Bloody hell, woman, I told you to wait for me!"

Clarissa turned to Brodie, confused. "You told me he was dying... but he is not... how?" Tears swam in her eyes. Then she felt dizzy, and the room spun, then she fainted.

Dalziel had just enough time to grab her and lift her into his arms.

He frowned at Brodie and seethed. "What did you do?"

"Brother, I can explain." Brodie had his hand palm up in front of him.

"You told her I was dying?" Dalziel roared.

"Och, I might have stretched the truth a little." Brodie winced.

"What did you do?" Dalziel asked, his voice cold.

Brodie seemed embarrassed now that he had an audience.

"I ken I did not think the entire plan through, but in my defense, I was trying to help."

Amelia was by Dalziel's side and feeling Clarissa's forehead. "I think she's had a fright, but she should come around soon."

Dalziel gently lay Clarissa on the bench as Amelia saw to her.

He then turned to Brodie and said, "You better tell me everything before I kill you."

Beiste cleared the room, then stood beside Dalziel. "Spill it, Brodie."

"I told Clarissa you were dying, and you were calling for her and Amelia thought you were at death's door."

"You imbecile!" Amelia huffed. "No wonder she looked terrified."

"You did what?" Dalziel growled.

Brodie took a few steps backward. "Now Brother, I meant well. I just wanted to prove Clarissa *still* loves you."

"By scaring her to death?" Dalziel lunged at Brodie, and Brodie took off, scrambling across the table to the other side.

"Calm down, Dalziel, twas well-intentioned. Clarissa dropped everything, scared out of her mind that you would die and not ken how much she loves you," Brodie replied. "Dinnae you see? It proves that she will take you back!"

"I'm going to kill you!" Dalziel shouted, then leaped across the table. Brodie sprinted to the other side, crashing over chairs to do it. He stumbled, then righted himself and headed for the door.

"You son of a bitch, come back here!" Dalziel was livid.

Brodie made it out the door and sprinted down the hallway, yelling for Dalziel to calm down. "I did it for you, Brother. I was trying to save *your* marriage. Dinnae kill me!" Brodie shouted just before Dalziel leapt onto Brodie's back and they both tumbled to the ground. Dalziel then planted his fist in Brodie's face.

It took Beiste and Kieran several minutes to pry them apart as they wrestled on the floor.

Later, when they sat outside the bedchamber where Amelia and Zala were attending to Clarissa. Dalziel had a bruised chin and Brodie nursed a black eye and split lip.

"Is she all right?" Dalziel asked when Amelia stepped outside. He stood immediately.

"Aye, she's as hale as can be, Dalziel. And she is asking for you."

"Wait... was it the shock? Is she well?"

"She is fine. Dinnae fash."

"But she fainted," he replied.

"Which is normal for a woman in her condition. Dinnae worry she and the bairn are fine."

"The bairn?" Dalziel appeared confused.

"Aye, tis most likely why she felt dizzy. She probably has not eaten and what with all the travel and the worry..."

"She is with child?" Dalziel whispered in awe.

"You did not ken?" Amelia asked.

"No." He felt a lump in his throat. Then a thought occurred to him. Dalziel glared at Brodie, who had a guilty expression on his face, having just learned Clarissa was with child.

"You dragged my wife halfway across the countryside while she is carrying my bairn!" Dalziel shouted with his fists clenched.

Brodie just said, "Shit!" and took off running.

Later, when everyone had calmed down again and Brodie now nursed *two* black eyes, he chuckled and said to Dalziel, "Och, now ye ken what it feels like, Brother, when someone interferes with your marriage."

Home

THAT NIGHT CLARISSA and Dalziel were in his bed, bathed, fed, and naked. They were also enjoying the third round of reconciliation coupling. Dalziel lay tied to the bed, fully aroused, while his wife loved him with her mouth. He cursed and gritted his teeth when she circled his tip with her tongue. Unable to move, he was completely at her mercy, something which was difficult for a dominant male like him.

Clarissa felt a heady sensation of complete power. She crawled up the length of him and placed a nipple across his lips. He suckled her, then she pulled away.

"Love, please have mercy. I need you," he rasped.

Clarissa did not make him wait. She straddled his hips, placed one hand on his chest for balance. With her other hand, she stroked his length and placed him at her center, then impaled herself on his hardened length.

Dalziel groaned and tried to break free. "Untie me, love. I want to touch you," he pleaded.

"Uh uh, Husband, there's no escaping me," she teased. With both hands on his chest, she rode him slowly, raising her hips and sinking down repeatedly, increasing the pace as she moaned loudly.

Dalziel lay on his back, his lids heavy with lust as he watched his wife ride. His length glistened with her arousal. He loved the sensual way she took her pleasure and how tight she felt wrapped around him. It took all his restraint to stop from exploding. He needed to take control.

Clarissa fastened her pace, and the exquisite feeling built. She closed her eyes and lost control, so much so she had not noticed that Dalziel had broken free of his restraints until she was flipped onto her back, and he was above her thrusting with abandon.

"I love you, Ris," he growled and licked her lips.

"I love you, Dalziel," she gasped, then bit his shoulder when her orgasm ripped through her. At the same time, Dalziel stiffened and joined her with his climax.

When they finally came down from their sensual high, Dalziel withdrew and rolled them onto their sides. No words passed between them. Just gentle kisses and caresses. Clarissa rested her head on Dalziel's shoulder and sighed with contentment because she was finally home.

Epilogue

Several months later - MacGregor Keep, Scotland

"No! No one touches her but Amelia. We will wait until she gets here," Dalziel growled.

"By the saints, you are an idiot. I have delivered many bairns with Amelia, and I recently gave birth to my second set of twins. Now move out of my way," Zala replied.

Dalziel stood across the doorway barring entry as Zala tried to get around him.

"Husband, move and let her... in!" Clarissa groaned the last word clearly in pain.

Dalziel looked stricken and ran to her bedside, abandoning the door completely.

Zala made her way inside with Jonet hot on her heels. A couple of maids came in with boiling water and fresh towels and bustled about the room.

Dalziel held Clarissa's hand, feeling completely helpless as she gripped it and squeezed when she was hit with another contraction.

Zala was on the opposite side and soothing her. "Tis all right, Ris, you can do this. Just breathe how we taught you."

Clarissa nodded, then threw her head back and clenched her teeth, moaning in pain.

"Where the hell is Amelia?" Dalziel shouted. He was already in panic mode and fearful for his wife.

"Wheesht, stop bellowing, you're scaring the fish down at the loch," Amelia replied as she strolled into the room. A basket was full of jars and plants and many healing items. As the clan healer, she was skilled and knowledgeable, and the only person Dalziel trusted with his wife. Hence why he insisted Clarissa give birth in Scotland under Amelia's care.

Dalziel held a relieved expression when she arrived. Amelia washed her hands and dried them, then greeted Clarissa. She set out her things, explaining the process to keep Clarissa calm.

Dalziel continued to hover over Clarissa as he remained to hold her hand.

Beiste peeked his head into the room, but stared down at the floor and asked, "Brother, do you wish to stay, or would you prefer to come with me and Brodie?"

"I wish to stay," Dalziel replied.

"He wishes to go," Clarissa said at the same time.

Dalziel glared at her and said, "I am staying."

Clarissa rolled her eyes and ignored him. She loved him to distraction, but he was getting on her fragile nerves with his hovering and constant bellowing.

"All right, if you need anything, just call. We will be down the hall." Beiste gave Amelia a knowing glance, then left.

Two hours later, Beiste and Brodie were called in to carry Dalziel out of the room because he had fainted, and he was getting in Amelia's way.

Although an assassin used to blood, it was all too much for Dalziel to see Clarissa suffer. He became light-headed and blacked out. Amelia said he could return just before the bairn arrived if he wanted to be present.

Several hours later, having recovered from his taxing ordeal, and after a couple of rounds of whiskey, Dalziel was by Clarissa's side, holding her hand, when his son finally came into the world, bellowing at the top of his lungs. When Jacob Cedric Robertson was placed in

Dalziel's arms for the first time, he kissed his teary-eyed wife, then *the Wolf* wept like a baby.

※

"AYE, WHEN YOU GROW up, you will become a fine warrior, just like your da. I will teach you everything you need to ken. Even dangerous things, but we willna tell your ma or she will worry," Dalziel whispered to his son.

He was sitting in a chair in the nursery rocking Jacob Cedric in his arms, trying to get him to go to sleep. Baby Jacob gurgled and smiled at Dalziel. His father's expression softened, and Dalziel bent down and reverently kissed his son on the forehead.

"Aye, you like the idea of keeping secrets from your ma. Well, dinnae worry, I ken all the tricks. You can learn from me." Jacob grinned and giggled, and Dalziel's heart melted all over again.

Clarissa had been standing in the doorway quietly watching her husband coo to their son. She loved these unguarded moments when Dalziel bonded with Jacob. Her heart filled to overflowing, watching the two people she loved most in the world share quiet moments together. Clarissa wondered how she had ever got so lucky finding a good man like Dalziel.

Suddenly, Jacob made a noise, and it sounded like "Da da." Clarissa gasped and ran into the room to sit beside Dalziel. She looped her arm in Dalziel's and held her son's hand.

Dalziel's entire face was awash with joy when he looked at her. "Ris! He just called me, Da!" Dalziel leant across and kissed Clarissa.

"Aye, I heard it," she said excitedly.

Then Jacob floored them both by saying, "Da... Da... Ma... Ma"

Clarissa and Dalziel gazed down with wide-eyed wonder at their son, who looked at both with pure adoration and love.

"Aye, we are your da and your ma, Jacob," Dalziel said. Then he and Clarissa proceeded to smother baby Jacob with laughter, hugs and kisses.

Clarissa savored the precious moment with her husband and her son. The love shone in her eyes whenever she looked at them and she knew she had it all. A love so deep and so profound she would cherish forever.

In that precious moment, Dalziel realized he had it all. Everything he ever wanted was right there in the room with him. All the darkness of his life vanished the moment he had Clarissa and Jacob by his side. They were his light, and he would love them forever.

1046 - MacGregor Keep, Glenorchy, Scotland

IT WAS CHRISTMAS TIME in the Highlands and the MacGregors gathered in the Great Hall, celebrating the birth of the Christ Child, and giving thanks for their abundant blessings. There was an abundance of food, wine, and music, and everyone was in high spirits. Most of the MacGregor clan were present from the War Band, retainers, and their families, to the crofters and villagers and Keep staff. The attendees on the main dais comprising the chieftain's immediate and extended family, including Amelia's grandfather, Gilleain Maclean from the Isle of Mull.

This Christmas, they had several recent additions. Beiste and Amelia MacGregor now had four bairns: Iona, Colban, Dalziel, and baby Moira. Brodie and Zala Fletcher also had four, two sets of twins. Thorfinn, Izara, Ajani and Abyssinia and Dalziel and Clarissa had two, Jacob and baby Cedric.

Sorcha was also present and very much unmarried, thanks to the overprotectiveness of her brothers, who scared off all her suitors. She was wondering if any man was brave enough to take on her big brothers. Little did she know soon, one man from a rival clan would not only have the courage to take on her brothers, but he would also steal her right out from under their noses.

Beth (Elsa) was also present with Jordie and agreed to attend once Clarissa assured her Arrowsmith would not be there. Beth had been avoiding Arrowsmith for weeks. While she allowed him time with Jordie, she maintained her distance. Their love story was a tragic one she dared not repeat. But it seems love was not done with them yet. Especially when the doors burst open midway through festivities, causing icy cold air to blast through the hall.

A Highlander crossed the threshold, covered in snow and wearing a long-hooded cloak. When he removed the hood, it was Arrowsmith. His blazing eyes scanned the room and when they rested on Beth, he growled and stalked towards her. She knew then the time for hiding was over.

As for King Macbeth *mac Findlaích*, earlier that year, he thwarted an attempt to dethrone him by Siward, the Earl of Northumbria. Because unbeknownst to Siward and Malcolm III, Macbeth already knew the attack was coming, thanks to the deadly cunning of *The Wolf*.

The End

Spin-off series, The MacGregors, continues with the story of Arrowsmith & Beth.
https://elinaemerald.com/books
Sign up for Elina's Newsletter & Free Story
https://dl.bookfunnel.com/aiq0ubhpx6
Buy Direct & Save
https://payhip.com/elinaemerald

Did you love *Pledged to the Wolf*? Then you should read *Arrowsmith*[1] by Elina Emerald!

Note: This is a spin-off novella to the Reformed Rogues series. Recommend reading series in order.

As the King's Man in the North, Ewan Arrowsmith walks a fine line between life and death. Deceit and treachery are his constant companions.

But there was a time, long ago, when he only knew truth and the love of a good woman called Beth. Their affair was brief due to a betrayal that led to tragedy. Years later, in a strange twist of fate, their paths cross again because of the interference of Clan MacGregor. Both have suffered in the intervening years. This time they must decide whether a second chance at love is worth risking everything.

---

1. https://books2read.com/u/4NXkOG

2. https://books2read.com/u/4NXkOG

Warning: Determined, brawny alpha male ahead and reluctant heroine. Occasional historical inaccuracies and frivolous entertainment. Not suitable for people under 18. It contains some mature content.

Read more at https://elinaemerald.com/books.

About the Author

Elina Emerald is a South Pacific-born Australian author who grew up in *Wiradjuri* and *Yuin* country.

A lawyer and research sociologist by trade, she spent several years songwriting and touring with an indie band. Elina developed a penchant for castles, old ruins, and medieval world history in her travels worldwide. She now writes Romantic Suspense books in different subgenres.

Read more at https://elinaemerald.com/.

CPSIA information can be obtained
at www.ICGtesting.com
Printed in the USA
LVHW041601150723
752291LV00037B/505